Andrea headed toward the backyard

At the first window she came to, she cupped her hands against the glass and peered in, but the view was blocked by stacked boxes. She continued to the back door, where she knocked loudly.

She banged on the door two more times. Finally, when it was clear no one was going to answer, Andrea grabbed the doorknob and jerked it sharply. As it had in her childhood, the latch opened. She shook her head. How many times had she and her sister snuck inside after curfew using that very same trick?

She called out. "Vicki? It's me. Are you in here?"

Andrea had been a paramedic for almost six years. She'd worked east Los Angeles and had gone into countless situations following 911 calls. Most of them were routine. Some of them were false alarms. But the minute she arrived on scene, she always knew if something was truly wrong. She wasn't sure how, but she could tell. The air vibrated in an odd way and even the light seemed different to her. Her co-workers had teased her at first, then had come to depend on her.

She was two steps into the kitchen when she froze.

Something in this house was wrong.

Very wrong.

Dear Reader,

When I was in the first grade, I stopped talking. This will come as a surprise to those who know me now, but it is the truth. My family moved in the middle of the school year, and after I joined my new class, where I knew no one and didn't really *want* to know anyone, I decided I would no longer speak.

My mother and father accepted the news with the same equanimity they gave almost every crisis in our household. No one got hysterical or rushed me to the doctor or even made a big deal out of my silence. I talked at home, you see; I just wouldn't say anything at school.

As the weeks went past and I continued my boycott on words, my mother, God bless her soul, sensed my loneliness. Every day in my lunch box I would find a note from her. As I ate my ham sandwich—always on white bread with the crusts cut off, please—I would read her letters.

Looking back, I ask myself, how did she have the time? My sister was in high school then, my brother in diapers. Surely she had more important things to do than write her stubborn seven-year-old love letters.

If you were to ask me why I did what I did, I wouldn't be able to explain, but by the end of that school year I decided to talk again. Thirty years passed before I learned other children do the same thing, and now there's even a name for the condition. It's called Selective Mutism. Strangely enough, all the articles I've read tell parents not to panic or make a big fuss. The experts say it will pass in time and it generally does.

When I sat down to write *Silent Witness* I knew I wanted to tell the story of a child who chose not to speak. In my book, Kevin has a much more traumatic reason to stay quiet than most children, but in a child's world, everything is relative.

I hope you enjoy reading this story as much as I enjoyed writing it.

Kay David

Silent Witness

Kay David

HARLEQUIN®

TORONTO • NEW YORK • LONDON
AMSTERDAM • PARIS • SYDNEY • HAMBURG
STOCKHOLM • ATHENS • TOKYO • MILAN • MADRID
PRAGUE • WARSAW • BUDAPEST • AUCKLAND

ISBN 0-373-71200-6

SILENT WITNESS

Carla Luan is acknowledged as the author of this work.

This edition published by arrangement with Harlequin Books S.A.

® and TM are trademarks of the publisher. Trademarks indicated with ® are registered in the United States Patent and Trademark Office, the Canadian Trade Marks Office and in other countries.

www.eHarlequin.com

Printed in U.S.A.

This is a special thank-you to all the dedicated teachers who have helped me through the years and continue to do so. Two in particular, Dan Chaney and Linda Winder, stand out because of their tireless efforts and endless patience. One taught me how to read and the other taught me how to write. I'll always be grateful.

Books by Kay David

HARLEQUIN SUPERROMANCE
798—THE ENDS OF THE EARTH
823—ARE YOU MY MOMMY?
848—THE MAN FROM HIGH MOUNTAIN
888—TWO SISTERS
945—OBSESSION
960—THE NEGOTIATOR*
972—THE COMMANDER*
985—THE LISTENER*
1045—MARRIAGE TO A STRANGER
1074—DISAPPEAR
1131—THE TARGET*
1149—THE SEARCHERS

*The Guardians

Don't miss any of our special offers. Write to us at the following address for information on our newest releases.

Harlequin Reader Service
U.S.: 3010 Walden Ave., P.O. Box 1325, Buffalo, NY 14269
Canadian: P.O. Box 609, Fort Erie, Ont. L2A 5X3

CHAPTER ONE

THEY SAY YOU CAN'T go home again. But invariably something draws you back to the place where you grew up.

Andrea Hunt turned her Jeep onto Beach Road and wondered what that something was. A desire for reassurance? A quest for lost youth? The chance to do things over?

She didn't know, but when she'd had to leave Los Angeles or lose her mind, Andrea had instinctively headed for Courage Bay. She had needed to heal her hurts and think about the direction her life should take. Home had been the only choice. The sparkling bay waters and sandy white beaches of southern California offered a refuge like no other.

Now, Andrea's older sister, Vicki, had followed her lead and come back to Courage Bay, too. And her situation was truly awful.

Andrea had to regroup, but Vicki had come back because her life had fallen apart big-time. She'd gone through a disastrous marriage, then an even more disastrous divorce and now she had no job, no husband and no plans. The only bright spot in her life, she'd told Andrea, was Kevin, her six-year-old son.

Turning right, Andrea drove up the steep road to the house where she and her sister had grown up. A few years back, their mom and dad had bought a home higher up one of the cliffs, but they'd kept the bungalow fully furnished and rented it. When Vicki had announced her homecoming, the place had been empty, and they'd insisted she take it for herself and Kevin.

For a second, Andrea considered how it would feel to live inside those cool stucco walls again. Like all the other paramedics in Courage Bay, she stayed at the fire station while she was on duty, her standard shift that of the fireman, twenty-four on and forty-eight off. For her free days, she had leased a tiny house that had come with an even tinier backyard and patio.

But it might be nice to have her own house someday. Along with her own family. And a husband who would never cheat on her.

She gunned the SUV and made it up the final hill, reminding herself to stay in the moment, the advice of her L.A. shrink echoing in her head. She had seen the doctor for several months right after her breakup with Brian, her latest—and biggest—mistake. The therapy had helped but Andrea wasn't fully convinced history wouldn't repeat itself; the only kind of men she seemed to hook up with were the wrong kind.

Pulling up next to the curb, Andrea parked her Jeep behind Vicki's still-packed Toyota and cut her engine. When she had phoned last night and volunteered to help her sister unpack, Vicki had eagerly accepted. She could use the extra hands, she had said. Then in her next breath, reverting to the roles they had each played before, she'd confessed she needed Andrea's advice even more.

The two sisters hadn't been close since Vicki had married. Although they'd both lived in L.A., distance and lifestyle had separated them, their personal and career paths taking them in completely opposite directions. When they'd talked, however, Vicki had sounded as eager as Andrea was to renew the relationship they'd had as kids. Back then, they had been almost inseparable, most strangers assuming they were twins because of their looks. The similarities had stopped there, though.

Unsure of herself and desperate to be popular, Vicki had constantly gone to Andrea for support and counseling, never quite sure of how to proceed, regardless of the fact she had been the older by two years.

Andrea had been just the opposite. Independent (exactly like their father, according to their mother) and stubborn (exactly like their mother, according to their father), she'd been the protector and leader.

Despite that background, Andrea didn't feel much in charge of anything these days and any advice she might give her sister would be questionable, at best. Especially where men were concerned, be they six or sixty-six.

She knocked on the front door, the screen banging under her knuckles as the sound of Mrs. Moore's wind chimes drifted over on a fresh sea breeze. The retired schoolteacher had been the Hunts' neighbor for as long as Andrea could remember. She had also been a constant source of sugar cookies for the two sisters. Andrea turned to see if the elderly woman's ancient Beetle was there, but her driveway was empty.

As empty, it seemed, as Vicki's house.

Andrea rapped on the door again, her impatience growing as she wondered why she was surprised. Unlike Andrea, Vicki never had trouble living in the moment. For her, the future was a vague concept and the past didn't even exist. Andrea loved Vicki but admitted that her sister could have just as easily woken up this morning and decided to take the bus back to Los Angeles.

Andrea left with a huff. Halfway to her Jeep, she started thinking and her footsteps slowed.

She was irresponsible and flighty, but Vicki really cared about Kevin. Reluctant to discuss all the details, she'd told Andrea over the phone he was one of the major reasons she had returned to Courage Bay. He had a problem, a serious problem, she'd said, and it needed to be addressed.

"Kevin stopped talking the day Grant walked out on us," she'd explained. "He talks at school, but he won't talk at home. To me. His teachers said the condition isn't *that* unusual and they even have a name for it. It's called selective mutism, but it's so frustrating…." Her voice had become bitter, an attempt to hide the obvious hurt. "I could kill Grant Corbin, Andie. This is all his fault! I should never have married that man!"

She'd gone on about the breakup of her marriage, the words spilling out in a rush she had been unable to contain.

"He cheated on me, Andie. He had a girlfriend and everything! When I found out, I went ballistic. She was a cop he worked with—redhead. I'm afraid Kevin knew what was going on even though I tried to keep it from him." She'd cursed again then continued fuming. "Grant just walked away. He never even came back to visit with Kevin. Never even called!"

Without further thought, Andrea returned to the house. Disregarding the front porch this time, she headed to the backyard. At the first window she came to, she cupped her hands against the glass and peered in but the view was blocked by stacked boxes. She continued to the back door where she knocked loudly, the faint sound of a radio lingering in the hot, stagnant air.

She banged on the door two more times. Finally, when it was clear no one was going to answer, Andrea grabbed the doorknob and jerked it sharply—to the right and down. As it had in her childhood, the latch opened. She shook her head and grinned. How many times had she and Vic snuck inside after curfew using that very same trick? They had always kept the hinges well-oiled but they squeaked loudly now as she stuck her head inside and called out. "Vicki? It's me, Andrea…. Are you in here? Hello?"

Andrea had been a paramedic for almost six years. She'd worked east Los Angeles and had gone into countless situations following 911 calls. Most of them were routine. Some of them were false alarms. But the minute she arrived on scene, she always knew if something was truly wrong. She wasn't sure how but she could tell. The air vibrated in an odd way and even the light seemed different to her. Her co-workers had teased her at first, then they'd come to depend on her.

She was two steps into the kitchen when she froze.

Something in this house was wrong.

Very wrong.

GRANT CORBIN HAD thought he would grow accustomed to the solitude, but a full year had passed since Vicki and Kevin had left and the place still felt empty and cold. He could never get comfortable, either. Looking around the half-empty room, he shook his head wryly.

Maybe if he had some furniture, things might be different.

Then again, maybe not.

Spending the money to replace what Vicki had taken had struck him as foolish and spending the time to select new things, impossible. Detectives in Los Angeles were usually short on the first and had none of the second, and Grant was no exception.

He crossed the living room and went into the kitchen, which was even less equipped for its purpose than the living room. The essentials were present, though, he told himself, reaching inside the refrigerator's freezer. When a man had a fifth of cold tequila, he didn't need anything more.

Perching on the one bar stool he'd kept, Grant twisted off the top of the bottle and took a long swig, holding the frigid alcohol in his mouth as he closed his eyes. He wished he could numb his brain as easily as he could his tongue, but it never worked that way. He'd tried, Lord knew he'd tried, but so far he hadn't found a bottle big enough to make that happen.

Opening his eyes, he swallowed and the freezing Cuervo slid effortlessly down his throat. Then he saw the bear.

The goddamn bear.

For some ridiculous reason he couldn't recall right now, he'd decided to clean the bedroom closets a week ago. He'd found the stuffed animal upside down on one of the shelves in the very back. He'd almost thrown it away, but then he'd remembered that the guys at the station kept some toys around to hand out when a child was brought in. Grant had fingered the tattered little bear, then set it on the kitchen counter to take with him the next day.

But the next day, he'd forgotten. And the day after that, he'd done the same. Finally, he'd been forced to admit the truth. He didn't want to get rid of the toy. He wanted to keep the damn thing because it was all he had left of Kevin.

Another mouthful of tequila went down, then he cursed out loud as the phone rang. He thought about ignoring its persistent call but he was a cop and cops didn't have that luxury. He picked up the receiver and grunted.

"Corbin? Get your ass down to the park. We got a dead gangbanger who was a bagman for Jaime Sanchez, that dealer over on Fourth who's been giving us hell. The first O says some of his buds are there and they want to talk."

Parker Richmond didn't bother to identify himself because he didn't need to. Another detective in

Hollenbeck, he and Grant had graduated from the academy at the same time and had been friends through four divorces, three lawsuits, and two near-miss gun battles, one a holdup that went bad and the other, a domestic that went violent.

"I just got home," Grant said.

"Then you still have your coat on." Parker's deep voice rang down the line. "C'mon, chop-chop."

Grant looked down. He did indeed still have on his coat.

"Screw you," he said pleasantly. "And the dirt-bag. I've got a cold bottle of Cuervo and I'm not going anywhere until I see the bottom of it."

"Then drink fast. I expect you here in fifteen minutes."

Parker hung up without another word, and Grant followed suit, rising to place the bottle back into the freezer with a pat. He and Parker both knew his protest had been automatic. He would take a murder any day of the week over a night at home by himself. Or a night out with friends, for that matter. Without a wife and kid, Grant no longer worked to live, he lived to work.

Passing by the teddy bear, he picked it up and held it to his nose. The little-boy scent he wanted to smell wasn't there so he brushed a knuckle over its plush back when he set it down. His steps were heavy as he closed the front door behind him.

ANDREA STOOD in the middle of the kitchen and listened to the silence around her. The radio had been playing music but now a taped commercial came on. She could only hear part of the words as the signal faded in and out. "…on the beach today…hope you've got that sunblock handy…another scorcher with a high of ninety-five and a low… The ozone level will be…"

Directly ahead of her, the kitchen opened up into the dining room and that area merged into the living room. If she turned left, she'd go down the hall that led to the bedrooms. She hesitated but only for a moment, her footsteps pulling her toward the large rectangular table on which her mother had served countless Sunday roasts.

The dark wood had a gloss so beautiful Andrea immediately knew her mom must have come over to clean. No one else could make the finish shine like that. The mirrored wall behind the buffet gleamed just as brightly. Glancing beyond the furniture to the wall of taped boxes beside the windows, Andrea read some of their haphazard labels. *Kit. Bed stuff. Toys.* If Vicki had unpacked anything last night, it wasn't in this part of the house. Andrea called out her sister's name again but no one answered.

When she entered the living room a second later, Andrea knew why. She gasped, her words half-curse, half-prayer. "Oh my God…"

Like a dinosaur that couldn't get up, her grandmother's huge mahogany armoire had fallen over. Its doors hung open uselessly, like broken limbs, their beveled inserts shattered, bits and pieces of molding and hardware strewn about the room as well as shards of broken glass.

All at once, a bit of white caught her eye. Underneath one of the cracked planks, something glowed, something with a small red bulb embedded in the center. When she realized what she was looking at, Andrea felt her knees wobble.

It was a shoe, a *kid's* tennis shoe, the kind with a little light on the heel that flashed when the child moved.

Only this light wasn't flashing.

Crying their names, she dropped to her knees to peer under the armoire. "Kevin? Vicki? Oh, God! Are you guys under there?"

She caught her breath as she heard a moan.

"Vicki?" she said, her voice high and frightened. "Is that you? Are you beneath the cabinet? Answer me!"

Her command was frantic but it elicited only silence. She tried again and got the same answer.

Rocking back on her heels, her gaze taking in more details, Andrea told herself to be calm. There had to be a way to get beneath the mess. She needed to do that first. After a second's study, she knew what to do. The chest was so big, it'd actually wedged itself against the opposite wall, about three feet up. If she was careful, she could climb over the top and worm her way underneath.

Her mouth dry, her pulse racing, she started forward, pieces of wood and broken glass crunching as she went. One careless move and she could create an even bigger disaster...but she had to get in there and get to Vicki and Kevin. She'd talked to her sister at nine last night. If this had happened right after they'd spoken, they could have been trapped for more than twelve hours!

Andrea inched her way to the place where the cabinet was propped against the stucco. She paused for a second and gathered her composure, then gingerly began to lower herself into the niche between the wall and the cabinet's side.

She tried not to breathe for fear of dislodging anything. As she slipped down, though, her belt hit the edge of the chest and for one heart-stopping second, everything seemed to groan.

After the debris settled, she tried again, making herself as skinny as possible and easing down—slowly—her back scraping against the rough plaster. If she'd been another inch wider, she wouldn't have fit.

Once inside the tiny crevice, she tucked herself into a tight ball and balanced on her haunches, leaning to her right to stare past her knees. A single ray of light had managed to pierce the darkness. Her eyes focused and she almost wished they hadn't.

The first thing she saw was her nephew. He lay motionless on his stomach three feet away, one leg trapped by a shelf, the other caught under one of the doors. Andrea whispered his name and his eyes fluttered open.

She swallowed and said, "Kevin, it's Aunt Andrea. I'm going to help you, okay? Before we get started, though, I need to know something." She took a deep breath. "Where's Mommy, Kevin? Is she behind you? Is she under there with you?"

He didn't speak. He simply raised one finger and pointed behind him.

Andrea leaned forward and craned her neck. The gloom was thicker where the case rested against the floor and she could see even less than she had before. Squinting hard, she edged another few inches closer and suddenly her sister's shadowy face emerged.

Andrea called her name. "Vic? Can you hear me? It's Andrea. Vic?"

Vicki stared back but she didn't answer. She couldn't.

She was dead.

CHAPTER TWO

DISBELIEF SLICED through Andrea. As an EMS tech, she'd delivered bad news to a lot of folks and their ability to protest reality had always baffled her. Now she understood their reaction because it was her own. She didn't *want* to acknowledge what she saw—she wanted to close her eyes and pretend her sister was alive.

But she couldn't. She saw far too many dead people in her job for any kind of denial to work.

Her gaze left Vicki's blank one and returned to the rubble. Shutting out everything else, she evaluated the scene like the professional she was.

From the placement of her sister and Kevin, it appeared as if the case had begun to fall and they'd been in front of it. Vicki had probably tried to warn Kevin because he was slightly turned, but he hadn't been able to get away. She'd caught the brunt of the weight and it'd taken her down.

A knot formed in Andrea's throat. Her sister had insisted on hauling the top heavy monstrosity from one place to another every time she'd moved. She'd even paid a fortune to have it fitted with special mounting strips to protect it in case of an earthquake. That was probably what she'd been doing—installing the strip to the studs—when the damn thing had gone over. It didn't make sense that something that large could tip over, but clearly it had.

Andrea looked at her nephew. His eyes were closed and in the somber light, he seemed dead, too. Except for the smudges on his face, his skin had no color and he hadn't moved since pointing to his mother. Turning her attention to his trapped legs Andrea tried to gauge the extent of his injuries. Her stomach clenched as she realized the cabinet's edge had missed him by an inch, an inch that had meant his life.

She stretched her fingers as far as she could, but she couldn't touch him. "Kevin? You need to wake up now, okay? You have to talk to me and tell me what hurts."

Vicki's explanation of his silences rang in Andrea's mind, but she had to think something this traumatic would jar him to speak.

"Kevin?" She raised her voice. "Kevin, can you hear me?"

His eyelids quivered for a bit, then he opened them and looked at her.

"Talk to me, sweetie," she pleaded. "Tell me

where it hurts. Besides your legs, does it hurt anywhere else?''

He stared at her with a strange kind of intensity and she felt as if he were trying to decide if she was one of the good guys or not. With the distance that had grown between her and Vicki, Andrea hadn't seen the little boy in more than a year, she realized with a catch. He was only six. Did he even remember her?

''I'm Aunt Andrea...your mommy's sister. Remember last Christmas? I'm the one who gave you the teddy bear. The little brown one with the black eyes.''

His gaze flickered but he didn't speak.

''Talk to me,'' she whispered. ''Please, Kevin... you have to talk to me.''

He stared at her for another long second, then he turned away.

Her frustration swelling, Andrea considered the possibility of moving him on her own, but she dismissed the idea quickly. It was too risky. The piece was too unstable and she didn't have the right equipment.

She had to have help.

Twisting awkwardly, she slipped her hand down to her waist. Her fingers found only her belt and she moaned in disbelief. Her cell phone wasn't there. Had she left the damn thing at home? Today of all days?

Then she remembered. When she'd edged in beside the armoire, she'd felt something give. It had to have been the phone's holster, not her belt, as she'd thought. Patting the floor to her right, she found only bits of wood. Repeating the action on her other side, her hand grazed the holder. She quickly wrapped her fingers around it, scared it might somehow move.

The operator answered before the first ring finished.

"Courage Bay Fire Department. Please state the nature of your emergency."

"Dispatch, this is Andrea Hunt, PRS, Squad One. I'm 10-7 but I need a unit for a 902 at 1425 Ocean View Drive, Code 3. I have a six-year-old juvenile down, possible broken ankle, possible internal injuries and one…adult…uh…926."

She stuttered over the radio jargon she'd rattled off countless times, the numbers stalling in her head, cold and harsh. Her big sister and 926, the code for a fatality. They shouldn't go together.

"Ten-twelve, Officer, while I call for unit."

Andrea stood by as the dispatcher instructed. She didn't want to look at Vicki again, but she couldn't help herself. The light had shifted and she could see more of her sister's face. It was untouched and exquisitely made up. Andrea guessed the accident had happened earlier that morning, but with Vicki, she couldn't be sure. All her life, her sister had kept her makeup fresh and perfect, looking as good at midnight as she did first thing in the day.

The operator's voice pulled Andrea back. "Units en route, Code 3 per your request."

"Ten-four." Andrea acknowledged the information then she closed the phone. Before she could decide what to do next, it rang. She answered instantly, an illogical fear swamping her that the noise might somehow cause the armoire to shift.

She answered, her voice shaky. "Hunt speaking."

"Andie, it's Alex! We caught the call and we're on the way. What the hell's going on? Isn't 1425 your parents' old place?"

Alex Shields was the captain of the other rescue squad and a close friend as well. Hearing his voice fueled a rush of relief—unfortunately it also made everything more real.

"It is their house," she said thickly. "I came over to help my sister unpack. She moved in yesterday, but when I got here, she didn't come to the door. I went inside and found...found my grandmother's armoire had fallen over. They're...they're trapped beneath it, Alex. Vicki and her son, Kevin."

"Oh, shit..." Over his curse, she could hear the sirens. "Andie...sweetheart...which one's the 926?"

"She is." Andrea swallowed hard then went on.

"Kevin is right beside her with both his legs stuck. I hope you've got a full crew. We're going to need it to lift this thing, then we have to get him to the hospital, full code."

"I'm bringing everyone, don't worry. Our ETA is five minutes, maybe less. Hang on, we'll be right there."

She hit the end key and looked over at her nephew. He had grown even paler. Holding her breath, Andrea scooted as close as she could. Her fingertips brushed his sleeve but he didn't respond when she called his name. She continued to try and rouse him even though she had the feeling it was pointless.

After a few minutes, he blinked and stared right at her. There were questions in his gaze…but they stayed where they were and remained unspoken.

WHEN SHE HEARD the sirens drawing near, a mix of relief *and* anxiety washed over Andrea. Courage Bay was not a large town. By this time, everyone at the Bar and Grill probably knew what had happened and it would be only a matter of time until her parents heard, too. She didn't want them learning the news of their daughter's death from a stranger but she couldn't call them now. Her phone had died a second after she had talked to Alex, the tumble from her waist apparently taking its toll.

She considered what their grief would be like,

then she pushed the thought away. Getting Kevin out took precedence over everything else, including anyone's sorrow.

Outside the siren grew louder and louder then ended abruptly, leaving only the rumble of the ladder truck's engine. When it shut down, a swell of men's voices replaced the momentary silence, Alex's deep baritone ringing out above the others. He was in charge of an engine crew of four, a ladder truck crew of five, and the other paramedic rescue squad, which had two members. He was also responsible for all their air rescues. It sounded as if he'd brought every person under his command. The only thing she didn't hear was the chopper.

Within minutes, they were on the front porch, Alex calling out for her.

"Break down the door," she cried. "I'm in the living room."

She gave the motionless Kevin another look, then eased up to stand against the wall. When the team entered and took in the situation, Andrea watched their expressions go from surprise to horror to determination. The Courage Bay Fire Department was comprised of professionals—they could handle anything and everything—but this was clearly something they hadn't seen before.

With a stunned expression, Rhonda Sutton, Andrea's partner in the ambulance they operated, lifted her eyes to Andrea's and slowly shook her head, her dark gaze filling with tears. A tall brunette with six men always at her feet, Rhonda had a reputation for being tough, but Andrea had seen underneath the facade. Rhonda cared deeply about their patients…and even more so for her friends.

Alex put the team into action, Andrea alerting them to Kevin's location as they planned how best to lift the broken cabinet. It seemed to take forever but in reality, only a few moments passed before they uncovered the little boy. He stared at the faces peering over him, his frightened eyes darting from the men to Andrea, then back again.

Finally able to get close, Andrea took Kevin's fingers in hers and started to reassure him, but then she found herself distracted. One of the men had brought in a blanket to cover Vicki. When he placed it gently over the still form of her sister, Andrea had to force her gaze back to Kevin's.

"It's okay, baby. These…these are the firemen who work in Courage Bay," she said. "They're here to help us."

Tightly gripping her hand, Kevin maintained his silence while they collared his neck and slipped the plastic backboard underneath him.

"You're very brave." Andrea walked beside the boy as they carried him out the front door. "I'm proud of you, Kevin. You're doing a great job!"

With smooth movements they'd made a thousand times, the men loaded the six-year-old into the am-

bulance and secured the stretcher. Andrea climbed
inside and kneeled down. "I'll be right behind you
in my truck, okay? When you get to the hospital,
I'll help them take you out. You aren't scared, are
you?"

He blinked then slowly shook his head. Brushing
back a lock of his hair, she kissed his forehead, her
throat stinging with tears she quickly swallowed.
"That's great because you have nothing to be afraid
of, nothing at all. Five minutes and we'll be there,
all right?" She jumped out and started to close the
double doors. A heartbeat before they slammed
shut, she thought she heard him say a single word,
but she hoped she was mistaken.

She had no idea how to answer when a child
cried out for his mother.

GRANT PEELED HIMSELF off the leather seat of his
white Impala and kicked the door shut behind him.
Crossing the steaming street toward Hollenbeck
Park, he lifted his sunglasses and blew his hair off
his forehead. The heat was suffocating and had
been for days. Demanding his attention like a dog
that wouldn't stop barking, the sun beat insistently
down against his neck, making it impossible to ignore. The jacket he'd had on was long gone, shed
in the car somewhere between Highway 101 and
South Soto.

He took a quick glance around the park as he

stepped over the curb. He hadn't thought to ask Parker where to meet him, but he realized now directions would have been superfluous. A crowd had already gathered at the South Boyle Avenue end of the green area, the usual mixture of old ladies, out-of-work men and kids who had nothing better to do. Grant named them derisively under his breath. They were ghouls, each and every one of them.

If there was a body around, they always showed up.

Having been warned more than once, Grant kept his insensitive label to himself and silently approached the group, removing his notepad and pencil as he walked. A sheet was over the body but the medical examiner lifted it as Grant reached his side. The face beneath the plastic was young. Too young to be so dead.

Standing nearby, Parker wiped his forehead. In his younger years, he'd been a full-back at UCLA. Now he was just plain fat, two-fifty if not more. The crazy heat wave they were having was about to do him in. He waved his hand toward the body. "You know him?"

Grant started to say no, then he kneeled and looked closer. "Yeah," he said. "I do know him. That's Tasha McKindrick's boy. I think they call him Poppy."

Parker yelled for one of the uniforms while Grant continued to stare. The boy couldn't have been over ten because his mother was only twenty-four. Grant had arrested her last year for selling drugs. They lived in one of the nearby projects with two younger children but no dad. Grant pulled the cover back over the boy's face and stood.

His stare lingering on the draped form at his feet, he thought of Kevin.

"What are we doing to our kids?" he muttered under his breath. "For God's sake, what in the hell are we doing?"

"What are *you* doing talking to yourself again? You promised me you'd given that up."

Grant raised his eyes to the woman who'd walked up beside him, her husky voice penetrating the gloomy fog of his thoughts. He hadn't heard her approach, but that's how Holly Hitchens did things. She snuck up on you, then pounced. They'd dated before he'd married Vicki and he had the scars to prove it. She was a hell of a cop, though.

"I make a lot of promises I don't keep." His eyes met hers and he shrugged. "You know how that goes...."

"I'm afraid I do. You always were lousy in that department, Corbin." Her answer was pure Holly but her voice sounded strained. Then he realized she wasn't looking him in the eye. Her gaze was usually so direct it hurt.

"What's up?" He made his voice casual and ignored the warning bells going off inside his head.

She took a deep breath and met his eyes. For a second he thought he saw pity in her gaze but that didn't make sense.

"I have some bad news, Grant."

Her use of his first name threw him even more. She'd always called him Corbin, even when they'd been lovers.

He tensed and she spoke again.

"Division just called looking for you and I told them you were here. They gave me a message to pass on. It's not good."

"What is it?" he asked levelly.

"Something's happened to Vicki. She…had some kind of accident down in Courage Bay."

"A car wreck?"

"No, it happened at her home, but I don't have any more details."

"But she didn't live in Courage Bay—"

"That's all they said. That she'd been there, in her house, and something fell on her."

"Is she okay?"

"No, Grant, she's not okay." Holly put her fingers on his sleeve. "I'm sorry, but she's dead."

Grant stared dumbly at the redhead, her words incomprehensible. Then something snapped in his hand. He looked down and opened his fist. The pencil he'd been holding was in two pieces.

Holly squeezed his arm. "There's more."

As a cop, he'd seen things that would test the

strongest stomach but Grant had never been affected. When Holly spoke, though, the ground beneath him shifted.

"Kevin?" he managed to get out.

"He was hurt, too. He's in the hospital at Courage Bay. They said he's not injured too seriously but—"

Grant didn't hear the rest. He was already running for his car.

ANDREA DECIDED her guardian angel must be working overtime. First, when she'd dashed back inside the house, she'd found Vicki's address book in the kitchen and had been able to contact Grant Corbin's office. Now, speeding to catch up with the ambulance, it seemed her luck was holding. Using the mobile phone she'd borrowed from Alex, Andrea released a sigh of relief when her father answered. Nine times out of ten, her mother was the one who picked up first, and Andrea wouldn't have been able to give her the news.

A retired Navy man, Jack Hunt was the rock of the family. The rest of them, including Karen, Andrea and Vicki's mother, depended on him. He started speaking before Andrea could say anything.

"Your mother's out shopping again," he said. "I swear, Andrea, I think she's determined to spend every dime I make! As far as an inheritance goes, forget about it. I know you won't need any help, but Vicki's another story. She's never been able to hold down a decent job and—''

''Dad... Dad, hold up for a minute, okay? I...I need to talk to you.''

He fell silent and Andrea told him what had happened. By the time she finished, she was crying, but he reacted as she'd expected. Stoic and in control. Only his voice gave him away and no one other than Andrea would have caught that.

''I'll find your mother,'' he said hollowly. ''We'll meet you at the hospital as soon as we can.''

''We're pulling in right now,'' she said. ''Look for me in the emergency room.''

Tossing the phone aside, she parked her Jeep and jumped out. Just as she reached the entrance, the ambulance driver wheeled Kevin's gurney through the E.R. doors at full speed. One of the trauma nurses, Jackie Kellison, ran to meet them, the newest E.R. resident, Amy Sherwood, right beside her.

Andrea explained the accident as the nurse and doctor rolled the child into one of the examining rooms. Without his mother or father present, Andrea had no legal basis to sign for his care but in Courage Bay, lives counted more than the rules.

''Tell me where it hurts, Kevin.'' Dr. Sherwood pressed her fingers against his belly while glancing down at his leg. When he didn't answer, she looked at him and repeated her question. When he still said nothing, she looked at Andrea.

"He's got some…communication issues." Andrea searched her rattled brain for the term Vicki had used and finally came up with it. "His mother said the condition's called 'selective mutism.'"

The resident nodded once, then without missing a step, continued her examination, talking to Kevin all the while as if she fully expected him to answer.

She was still poking and prodding when Andrea's parents bustled into the room.

Karen Hunt's slim figure and blond highlights usually hid her real age of sixty, but the news of Vicki's accident had added years. Her eyes were frantic and wild, her face pale and lined. Even her clothing was disheveled—she'd clearly changed before they'd rushed to the hospital and her blouse was misbuttoned.

She caught Andrea's eye and shook her head minutely, a silent understanding passing between mother and daughter. This wasn't the place for them to cry and console each other. Not in front of Kevin. For his sake, they had to stay in control of themselves. Nothing meant more than him right now, including their own grief.

Andrea acknowledged the message then moved away from the bed so they could get closer. Her mother grabbed Kevin's fingers and began to talk to him softly, Jack Hunt going to the other side of the bed to place a beefy hand on the child's shoulder.

Andrea slipped into the corridor, leaned against the wall and closed her eyes.

GRANT COULDN'T REMEMBER the last time he'd been to Courage Bay. Speeding south from L.A., the Impala pushed to its limit, all he could think about were the times he hadn't come.

The Hunts' twentieth anniversary. Christmas two years ago. Vicki's birthday the first year they'd been married.

She had wanted to visit Courage Bay more often, but each time they'd tried, his job had seemed to interfere. Vicki hadn't bought his explanation that murderers didn't take off on holidays. She'd accused him of manufacturing excuses, saying he didn't want to go with her because he hated her family.

She'd been half right. Sometimes he had used work as an excuse, but not the way she thought.

His problem was actually the opposite of her complaint. He loved Karen and Jack Hunt but in the L.A. world he'd come to consider his own, people like them just didn't exist. Years of working Vice and now Homicide had made him forget how to act around moral and sane individuals. The only way he could deal with the situation seemed to be by avoiding them.

Then there was Andrea. Vicki's little sister.

The first time he'd met her, he'd been shocked. He'd never seen two individuals, including twins, who resembled each other so strongly.

A striking woman with thick honey-colored hair and dark-blue eyes, Vicki had brought the JP's office to a standstill the day they had walked in to get married. Grant had felt eyes on him, too, everyone wondering why in the hell someone like her would be marrying someone like him. Andrea shared that beauty but there was more to her than there had been to Vicki, something deeper, something darker.

After he'd gotten to know her a bit, Grant had relaxed enough to hold a decent conversation with Andrea, but he'd always found himself wondering if she'd feel the same, kiss the same, make love the same…as Vicki. He knew his disquiet came from somewhere other than just the uncanny resemblance the two women shared yet he hadn't wanted to examine his reactions too closely. He had been married to Vicki, after all.

In the end, he had let his wife visit her family alone. They had all been so happy to see Kevin, no one had really noticed his father was absent and that had been fine with Grant.

He gripped the steering wheel and prayed the little boy would be okay. Kids had never figured much in Grant's life until Kevin had been born, then he'd begun to understand what all the fuss was about. Despite the circumstances, Grant couldn't have possibly loved Kevin any more than he already did—it had damn near killed him when they'd packed up and left.

Kevin had been four, almost five, at that point. Grant shook his head. Where had the time gone? He and Vicki had been divorced a bit more than a year and Grant hadn't seen Kevin once during that time. Would he even remember who Grant was? Would he still throw his arms around Grant's neck and hug him tight?

Grant had expected little from his marriage, and he hadn't been disappointed. He'd known the score from the very beginning, however, and he had no right to complain. Vicki could have had any man on the planet yet she'd picked him. He still didn't know why but he no longer cared, either. Kevin was all that mattered.

Reaching the outskirts of Courage Bay, Grant realized that his love for Kevin was all he had left. With sudden resolve, he promised himself he'd take care of this once and for all. He'd be the kind of father the little boy deserved.

And *that* was a promise Grant Corbin would keep.

CHAPTER THREE

ANDREA'S MOTHER AND FATHER stood by the edge of Kevin's gurney while his doctor and the hospital's orthopedic surgeon discussed his situation. At the foot of the bed, Andrea listened, as well. The two physicians came to a consensus quickly. An operation might be necessary, but it would be simple and straightforward, a matter of aligning Kevin's bones. Pending the outcome of the X rays, they might even be able to avoid surgery completely.

The radiation technician came to take the child for his tests and Jack leaned over his grandson. "I think I'll come along with you, big guy," he said. "If you don't care, I'd like to see how they do this."

Kevin blinked twice and his expression cleared. He couldn't have spoken and made his relief more known.

Andrea watched them leave, her mother at her side.

"We might as well go to the cafeteria and get

something to eat,'' Andrea said. ''He'll be in X ray for a while. I'll tell the nurses where we are and they can come get us.''

Taking off the mask of cheerfulness she'd put in place for Kevin's sake, Andrea's mother let her features collapse into the shell-shocked expression she'd worn earlier. She held up her hand at Andrea's suggestion and shook her head. ''No. No food. I don't want anything to eat. I want a cigarette.''

Karen Hunt hadn't smoked in ten years. Andrea opened her mouth to protest but she swallowed her words. They all needed whatever help they could get, wherever they could find it.

They walked across the street to a convenience store and bought a package of cigarettes, returning a few minutes later to the benches near the ambulance bay doors. Her mother lit up while Andrea sat in silence.

Karen Hunt smoked with determination, repeatedly drawing on the cigarette until she started to cough. After a bit, she dropped the butt, ground it beneath her heel, then looked at Andrea. There was steel in her voice. ''Tell me what happened. And I want the truth.''

Andrea gave her mother as many details as she could remember. ''I didn't have time to check before we left,'' she said as she finished, ''but I think Vicki was probably trying to anchor the armoire to

the wall and that's when it went over. It always was
unstable and top-heavy.''

Her grief segued into anger and she hit the bench
with her fists. ''I *told* Vicki it was silly to cart that
damn thing all around the state. She should have
left it—''

Her mother, revealing a strength that surprised
Andrea, reached out and covered Andrea's clenched
hands. ''Drop it, Andrea. The reason the armoire
fell over isn't important. What matters is that…''
She paused and drew a shaky breath. ''What matters is that Vicki is gone. What she'd want us to do
now is take care of Kevin. That's what we have to
concentrate on. Kevin.''

Andrea struggled to pull herself together. The effort took the last of her energy. ''You're right,''
she said. ''You're right…. In fact, Kevin's the first
thing she mentioned when I called and offered to
help her unpack. She said she'd take the help, but
she needed advice regarding him more than she
needed anything else.''

Her mother nodded. ''About his silence?''

Andrea stared at her mother in surprise. ''You
knew?''

''Vicki told me of the problem several months
back. I advised her to talk to a therapist.''

''Why didn't you tell me?''

''Vicki asked me not to say anything.'' Her
mother wrapped both hands around her package of

cigarettes, then looked into the distance. "She was upset. She felt it was her fault for being a bad mother and said you'd never have a problem so lame and she didn't want you to know. I guess her concern for Kevin finally overran her embarrassment and that's why she told you."

Andrea felt her mouth drop open. "But Vicki *was* a good mother! And I would never have said anything regardless of—"

Karen Hunt held up her hand. "I know that and you know that, but Vicki didn't. She was very insecure, Andrea. She always looked up to you. She thought you were perfect."

"Perfect? Me? Oh, God…" Andrea buried her face in her hands. "Why on earth would she think that?"

"Mrs. Hunt?"

A voice broke through Andrea's anguish. She looked up to see a woman from the front office approach her mother with an outstretched hand.

"I'm Wendy from Intake. We need some information about Kevin and since his father isn't here yet and his mother…is gone, I need your help. If you could come with me…?"

Andrea's mother jumped up from the bench and followed the woman back inside. Feeling numb and empty, Andrea sat quietly, the thought of Vicki fretting over her so-called "perfection" too much to even comprehend. The idea was ridiculous.

Andrea was far from perfect. Very, very far.

GRANT HURRIED toward the double doors of the Courage Bay E.R., the pavement beneath his feet steaming from the sun's steady heat. A thousand scenarios ran through his head as he walked, none of them good. They fled his consciousness, however, when a flash of motion off to one side caught his eye. He turned and looked closer, suddenly thinking Holly had been wrong.

Vicki wasn't dead. She was right there, twenty feet away.

A millisecond passed, then he realized his mistake.

He was looking at Andrea.

She wore a pair of white shorts and a red T-shirt, her thick hair pulled back haphazardly, her face free of cosmetics. Obviously prepared for nothing more than an average day at home, she looked devastated by what had happened, her slumped posture reflecting her state of mind, her gaze directed toward the ground as if it held some cosmic secret.

As he continued to stare, she raised her head. Across the grassy slope that separated them, their gazes converged.

Nothing dramatic or heart-stopping occurred. Grant didn't feel a jolt of awareness or a tingle down his spine. His heart didn't leap out of his chest or even jump at all.

He merely felt empty.

Vicki Hunt had manipulated him and used him, then she'd sent him on his way. He'd known exactly what she was doing and he'd been a willing victim, but that didn't mean it hadn't hurt. He would have thought the old pain might surface upon seeing Andrea, but apparently it'd sliced through him cleanly, albeit all the way to the bone. He felt nothing at all.

Changing directions, he headed toward her and she stood as he came near. Up close her feelings were even more apparent, but instead of the grief he expected, Grant saw anger on her face. He wasn't too surprised—people handled death differently.

Her voice was hoarse and throaty. "You got my message, I see."

Grant didn't waste any time. "How is he? Can I see him?"

"They're still checking for internal injuries. Kevin's in X ray right now. When he finishes there, you can probably see him, but that's going to be a while longer."

"Tell me what happened."

She recited the basic facts in a dry and emotionless manner. He could tell she'd already told the story more times than she wanted.

The minute she stopped speaking, questions flooded his mind but Grant stayed silent, approaching the situation the same way he did everything in his life—as if this was an investigation he was about to undertake. He'd gather the facts, study them, *then* proceed.

He realized belatedly she was waiting for him to comment. "I came as quickly as I could," he said awkwardly.

Her gaze was steady. "That's nice. But I only called because I thought you should know what had happened. I can handle the situation."

"I'm sure you can handle just about anything, but—"

"I can," she reiterated. "You should have phoned first and I would have saved you the trip."

"'Saved me the trip'?" He repeated the words carefully. "I don't believe I understand."

"The way Vicki explained things, I didn't think you'd care that much, one way or the other."

Doubting Vicki had employed the truth in her explanation, Grant cursed under his breath. The real story could take her down as efficiently as it could him.

"Why don't you tell me exactly what your sister said?" Grant said. "It might make things easier."

"It might," she conceded. "But I don't intend to share her confidences. I think it'd be best if you left."

"I'm not going anywhere. Kevin is my son."

"That's stretching it a bit, don't you think?"

Grant put on a rigid mask, his chest going tight. "What are you implying?"

"I'm not implying anything. I'm making a point. You left Vicki and Kevin. You abandoned them. That's not the kind of thing a loving father and husband does to his family."

His relief outweighed the sting her words brought with them. Still, a dilemma remained. Should he go along with the assessment and look like an asshole or try to convince her that Vicki had lied? Either way, he'd lose.

He stalled. "Is that what Vicki told you? That I abandoned them?"

Andrea stared at him without answering.

"Well, I guess that answers that," he finally said. "You've made up your mind. I won't try to confuse you with the facts."

IN THE FOUR YEARS Grant Corbin had been married to her sister, Andrea had talked to the man maybe half a dozen times. On the rare occasions when everyone managed to shake free from their busy lives and meet in Courage Bay for a family get-together, something seemed to come up at the last minute that kept Grant from attending. Each time, Vicki had excused him by saying crimes weren't scheduled, but Andrea had always wondered.

Now she wondered even more. Accustomed to

facing the unknown and dealing with whatever arose, she still felt a nameless anxiety building.

He was lying to her and she had no idea why.

"My sister gave me the facts. I know what happened."

"I doubt you know it all…." he retorted. "There were things I did that I shouldn't have, but the same could be said for Vicki. I love Kevin, though. Surely she didn't say that wasn't the case."

Andrea started to answer, then heard her name. She turned to see her mother standing by the E.R. door.

"The doctor's here," she called out. "He wants to talk to us." Seeing Grant, Karen Hunt motioned for them both to come.

They walked in uncomfortable silence to the door. Grant reached out for the handle but instead of opening it, he paused and looked at Andrea. She saw with shock that he had pain in his eyes.

"Look, before we go in, I have to ask you a question." His whole body seemed to tense. "Can you put everything else aside for a minute and answer it?"

"What is it?" she asked stiffly.

"When you found Vicki…did it look like, well—"

Surprised he even cared, she instantly understood the question; she'd heard it asked more times than she wanted to remember.

''She didn't suffer,'' she said quietly. ''I have a feeling the whole thing happened very quickly.''

Sympathy pushed past her anger as he flinched. He then nodded and opened the door and they went into the waiting room together.

To Andrea's amazement, her mother and father both greeted Grant warmly, Karen wrapping an arm around his waist and hugging him tightly, Jack extending his hand. Vicki had obviously not told their parents what she'd told Andrea. Infidelity wasn't a fault either of them would have brushed off.

Drawing Andrea's attention away from her thoughts, the orthopedic surgeon began to speak. ''The first X rays are back and I think we're going to be able to avoid operating on Kevin's foot at this point. He has a malleolar fracture but we can immobilize it with a plaster cast and that might do the trick....'' His explanation continued, his words filling Andrea with relief. A broken ankle bone was a far cry from the internal injuries she'd been worried about.

Andrea's gaze sought Grant's. He had dark eyes, so dark they almost seemed black. She couldn't read the emotions he hid, but she could feel them, their negativity seeking her out. He didn't like her, she realized with a shock.

The knowledge unsettled her, but she decided swiftly it didn't matter. The feeling was mutual.

STANDING BY ONE OF THE big windows in the emergency waiting room, Grant watched Karen and Jack Hunt leave a few minutes later. Now that they knew their grandson would be all right they had to deal with the sad details of their daughter's death. Andrea walked beside them but she was going to return. She'd told him so and asked him to wait for her.

Grant turned away from the glass. He'd thought at first that Andrea had known everything but he decided he'd been wrong. Vicki had informed her sister of what she'd wanted to, making him sound like the jerk and her the golden princess. He didn't really care what Andrea Hunt thought of him but he didn't want her for an enemy. That wouldn't be a good idea.

When she came back, she'd been crying. Her eyes were red-rimmed and wet, but she put aside her grief. "Let's go to X ray," she said. "You can see Kevin if they haven't begun the cast."

Grant wanted to say something about Vicki as they headed down the hallway, something appropriate and normal, something that ordinary people might say to one another when someone died, but he'd been out of polite society for so long, he'd lost the rule book. He didn't know how to act around women like Andrea.

Staring at the floor as they walked, he finally said the only thing he could think of to say.

"I'm sorry about all this," he said in a low voice. "I know you and Vic were close when you were kids. She talked about you a lot."

He was an expert at reading reactions—if a good Vice cop wanted to live to be an old Vice cop he picked up the skill quickly. Andrea was taken off guard by his words; her voice reflected her reaction and so did her body.

"She talked about me?"

"All the time. She wanted to be more like you."

Her response was so softly spoken he barely caught it.

"Well…shit…"

He raised an eyebrow.

Her hair shimmered as she shook her head. "Why on earth would she feel that way? I'm not hero material, believe me."

"Vic thought so."

"Well, she thought wrong." Her voice sharpened and so did her look.

Raising his hands defensively, he backed off. "Fine…she thought wrong."

The elevator dinged and the doors opened. Without a word, Andrea Hunt stepped inside and Grant entered as well. An eternity later they arrived on the next floor and they escaped, the silence between them thick and full of tension. Andrea didn't stop until she came to a doorway that had a "Radiation" sign above it and a sliding glass window set beneath. When it rolled back following her knock, Andrea talked to someone inside, then she turned and tilted her head toward the door.

"He's finished," she said. "We can see him but only for a second."

Kevin was lying on a gurney just inside the doorway, looking pale and frightened. Grant felt his heart turn over and calling the boy's name, he hurried to the bed.

Kevin's eyes opened slowly then widened when he saw Grant. A smile lit up his face.

Grant wanted to pick him up and whisk him away but he settled for a hug, burying his face in Kevin's neck and breathing in deeply. The flood of emotions that followed rocked him. How could he have let this kid go? What had he been thinking?

Pulling back, Grant studied Kevin from head to toe. When he finished, he shook his head. "How'd this happen, buddy? Are you okay? Does anything hurt?"

He waited for the little boy to answer him but Kevin stayed silent. Grant looked toward the foot of the stretcher where Andrea waited. She said nothing, either.

"Kevin?" Grant asked again. "Did you hear me? What happened, son?"

When Kevin answered with only a stare, Grant turned away from the child and moved to Andrea's side. She had a small scar beneath her right eyebrow, he noticed, a thin pale line that ran from there across her temple.

"What the hell's wrong with him?" he whispered tightly. "Why won't he answer me?"

"I thought you knew," Andrea murmured, her voice so low he could barely hear it. "Didn't Vicki tell you?"

"Vicki didn't tell me jackshit." He sent a confused look in Kevin's direction, his heart tripping, then he faced Andrea again. "What's wrong with him?"

"Kevin doesn't talk anymore," she said quietly. "He's been mute since the day you left."

CHAPTER FOUR

THE SHOCKED LOOK ON Grant Corbin's face was
genuine. He'd had no idea of Kevin's problem.

He started to say more, then halted, obviously
deciding not to discuss the situation in front of his
son. Surprised by the show of sensitivity, Andrea
rejected her momentary flash of appreciation. She
didn't want to see anything positive in the man
who'd broken her sister's heart.

Grant spoke with Kevin a little longer, then
stepped away from the gurney. Andrea took Grant's
place and kissed her nephew's forehead. "We're
going to another part of the hospital now, Kevin,
and the doctors are going to put a cast on your foot.
When that's done, we'll go upstairs to a room that
will be yours while you're here. We'll be right behind you, okay?"

The nurse came and began to roll the bed down
the hall, chatting to the little boy as she pushed him
along. In the cast room, Andrea and Grant got
Kevin settled, then the tech arrived. The young man
quickly started a monologue on the merits of dif-

ferent computer games. Apparently well-versed in what kept the interest of kids with broken bones, he tilted his head toward the door a second later. Andrea and Grant took the hint and went into the corridor, the nurse telling them to come back in an hour.

Grant ran his hands through his straight dark hair. "God. I had no idea—" He stopped abruptly and looked at her. "Can we get out of here? Hospitals and I don't get along too well."

Curious but unwilling to ask him why, Andrea shrugged. They retraced their steps to the E.R. exit and went outside to the bench where Andrea had been sitting before. The fresh air and sunshine felt wonderful after the antiseptic smell of the hospital, but strangely enough, they also seemed to trigger her grief. As soon as she took her seat, the sorrow she'd been holding off washed over her. Vicki was gone. Her one and only sister was dead.

Her tears came in a hot wave.

Grant made no attempt to touch her or console her or voice some useless platitude, and once again, she found herself, unwillingly, impressed by his actions. He didn't seem like the kind of guy who could sense what people needed, but his actions gave him away.

After longer than she would have liked, Andrea managed to pull herself together.

Handing her a white handkerchief, Grant gave

her another minute, then he spoke. "What in the hell is going on with him?"

Taking a deep breath, Andrea looked up. "I thought you knew he'd been having trouble."

"Vicki didn't—" Once again, he stopped himself. "I didn't know anything about it," he said simply.

"Neither did I," Andrea said, "but when I called Vicki the night before the accident, she said Kevin had stopped talking to her after the divorce. Apparently, he would talk at school, but not to her. She discussed the situation with a counselor and his teachers. They call the problem 'selective mutism.' They recommended therapy and told her not to make a big deal out of it. A lot of times children who have this condition apparently resume talking and no one ever finds out why they stopped in the first place."

"Has he spoken to you?"

Andrea shook her head. "Not so far."

"What about your parents? Did he talk to them?"

"No."

Grant tightened his jaw, then looked at her. "Why didn't I know this?"

"You would have if you'd gone to see him."

His expression was rock-hard and she swallowed uncomfortably.

"I tried," he said. "But Vicki always had a reason I couldn't."

"That's not what she told me."

"Vicki and I didn't see eye to eye about a lot of things, but I loved Kevin." He spoke tightly, his tension obvious in the set of his broad shoulders. "And I still do," he added.

With an effort she knew was visible, Andrea regained her coolness. "Are you calling my sister a liar?"

"I'm saying there are two sides to every story. I have a feeling you're going to need to remember that in the coming days."

His warning startled her. Vicki had never truly deceived Andrea, but she had had a penchant for twisting the truth, especially about things that might put her in a bad light. Andrea pushed that to the corner of her mind and concentrated on the present.

"All I have to worry about in the coming days is my nephew," she answered curtly. "He's my top priority."

"And mine, too."

"Then we'll stay in touch with you." The promise was hard to make but Andrea had to do the right thing. That was how she'd been raised. "I'll make sure you know how he's doing."

"I'll keep abreast of his progress by myself," Grant said in an equally cool voice. "I have no intention of going anywhere until my son has healed and I can take him home.''

Grant's ominous words paralyzed her without warning. She felt like an idiot, but until this very second she'd never considered the fact that Grant might want Kevin. After everything Vicki had said, Andrea had just assumed the little boy would become the responsibility of the Hunt family. *Please, God,* she thought suddenly, *please tell me I'm misunderstanding this.*

''What about your work?'' she asked. ''Don't you need to get back to L.A.?''

''I haven't taken a vacation in five years. LAPD will keep going without me.''

''But what about—''

''He's *my* son, Andrea.'' Grant cut off her words, any hope she might have harbored about the situation destroyed by his steady stare. ''I don't know what your problem is, but you're not going to get rid of me. I'm staying here. I love Kevin and I intend to make sure he knows that. I'll be taking care of him from now on.''

GRANT LEFT ANDREA sitting in the hot sunshine and walked back toward the E.R., her shocked expression telling him everything he needed to know. And more.

True to form, Vicki had made Grant the bad guy, the one who'd been responsible for the breakup of their marriage. He shouldn't have expected anything less, but somehow this final betrayal hurt more than the ones before. Maybe because he knew there was no way he could correct it. Vicki was gone and the truth of what had happened between them had died with her.

The automatic doors swished open, and Grant made his way to the phone hanging on one wall.

He called his captain first and explained what had happened. "I may need to take some time off—"

His boss responded just as Grant had thought he would. "Take whatever time you need, Corbin. The department understands—"

Grant gruffly thanked the man then broke the connection to dial a second number.

Parker answered on the third ring and once again, Grant gave out the details of Vicki's death. He finished by saying, "Listen, Park, this may take a while to figure out. Can you hang in there for a week or so without me?"

"Hey, no problem." His partner answered without any hesitation. "You do what you need to, Grant."

"Thanks, man. I appreciate it."

Relieved to have those two calls out of the way, Grant hung up the phone, turning as he did so. Andrea was still sitting where he'd left her, the sun blazing down on her. As he stared, she crossed one slim leg over the other.

The graceful movement was so reminiscent of

Vicki, his heart flipped. Like a line of falling dom-inos, that motion then triggered another reaction. When he could breathe again, he told himself he was going nuts, but an immediate disquiet had flooded him. Vic had traveled in circles she shouldn't have and had known folks he'd wished she didn't. Some of them had been dangerous and influential. He'd warned her of the consequences that came with hanging around those people, but she'd blown him off, saying she could take care of herself.

Time and time again, he'd witnessed the down-fall of the poor SOBs in the department who couldn't turn loose of their ex-wives. He hadn't wanted to be one of those pathetic men, but the unease Grant felt now went far beyond that.

Could there be a link between Vicki's death and those powerful people? Highly unlikely, he decided a moment later. Too risky.

Andrea stood up, catching his gaze as she wiped her eyes. His thoughts hop-skipping, he found him-self wishing Vicki had told her sister the truth, but he quickly realized what that would mean and he pushed the thought aside.

The truth was the last thing he wanted Andrea Hunt to know.

WITH GRANT by her side, Andrea headed back into the E.R., resolved to the fact that he was staying in

Courage Bay but still very unhappy about the situation.

She tried to remind herself the man *was* Kevin's father and it was only fair that he would want to be there. But she didn't want "fair."

Kevin's bed was empty when they arrived but five minutes later the door opened to reveal Kevin's gurney. Grant and Andrea jumped up in unison and ten minutes after that Kevin was settled into his bed, his cast an awkward appendage he didn't quite know how to handle. Andrea fussed around him, fluffing his pillows, getting him ice and turning on the television. From his chair in the corner, Grant watched her in silence, his steady gaze making her even more nervous. Finally, as Kevin dozed, Grant came to the side of the bed where she was adjusting the railing. Again.

He put his hand on her arm. "Why don't you go home?" he said quietly. "I'll be right here with him. You need to slow down and catch your breath."

His touch burned. "I'm perfectly all right," she protested, trying to ease her arm away without being obvious about it. "I want to be here—"

She cut off her protest when the door opened unexpectedly. With relief, she saw Alex standing on the threshold. Andrea went to him in two steps, giving him a hug then introducing him to Grant.

The two men shook hands in a measured way, exchanging a look as well. Andrea puzzled over the moment, but it passed so quickly, she decided she'd imagined it.

"How you doing, Kevin?" Walking to the end of the bed, Alex nodded to the little boy who'd come awake at the commotion. "That's a cool cast."

Andrea answered for Kevin. "The doctor says he fractured one of his malleoli, but the cast should take care of it. The X rays look good, other than that."

"Great news…" Alex put one of his fists on top the other then swung them together, as if he were batting a ball. "You get out of here, we'll go out to the little league field and knock some balls around. Sound fun?"

Kevin nodded, his eyes drooping with exhaustion. A second later, he was sound asleep.

They tiptoed into the hall, Alex shaking his head. "Man, when I walked in that house and saw what had happened, I couldn't imagine anyone surviving under the mess. I'm glad he's okay." He turned to Andrea and gave her another quick hug. "But I'm sorry about your sister." He faced Grant next. "Real sorry. I know you'll both miss her."

Andrea nodded because it was all she could do. They chatted for a few more minutes, then Alex said his goodbyes. As the firefighter started down the corridor, though, Grant spoke up unexpectedly.

"Alex—wait. I think I'll get some coffee. Can you show me where the cafeteria is?"

Pausing midstride, Alex grinned over his shoulder. "Sure thing. I won't guarantee you'll want to drink the coffee, though. Hospital food is hospital food...."

Her nervousness suddenly blooming, Andrea crossed her arms, leaned against the wall and watched the two men leave. The minute they turned the corner, she groaned out loud.

Grant was up to something. The only question was what.

THEY RODE THE ELEVATOR down, the tall fireman talking easily about nothing important. Grant knew a lot of men like Alex Shields; he'd grown up around them because his father had been a cop. The officers in Grant's Homicide division were like Shields, too, for the most part. Gregarious, outgoing, friendly types. Grant didn't know why he was so different from them, but he was. All those years in Vice had a lot to do with it, he was sure, but it went deeper than that. In the end, he'd found himself more comfortable in that life than his real one, and that's when he'd had to leave it.

They reached the first floor and Alex pointed to the left. "The cafeteria's right down there. You can't miss it—just follow your nose.'' He stuck out his hand but Grant didn't take it.

''Are you in a hurry or do you have a minute?'' he asked instead. ''I'll buy you a cup if you've got the time.''

The fireman hesitated.

''I'd like to ask you a few questions,'' Grant explained. ''About Vicki and the accident. I need some details but I didn't want to bother Andrea. I didn't want to upset her.''

Shield's frown cleared. ''Of course,'' he replied. ''I'll help as much as I can.''

His words confirmed the assumption Grant had made when Shields had come in the room and Andrea had greeted him. They were more than just friends, good or otherwise. Grant filed the information away for later examination.

They got their coffee then sat at a small table near the window, Grant wishing his cup held something stronger. He took a single sip and set the mug aside. It'd been nothing but an excuse anyway.

''I want you to tell me what you saw when you went inside Vicki's house.'' He sat back in his chair, fully aware he wore what Parker called his ''interrogation'' look. Intense, dark, focused. ''Tell me any details you can remember, no matter how small.''

Shields faced him squarely. ''I saw a hellacious

mess,'' he answered. ''That armoire weighed a ton—your son was lucky as hell he didn't die, too.''

''Did it look like they'd been moving the thing?''

''Hard to say exactly,'' the fireman answered with a shrug. ''The bottom of the piece was out from the wall about a foot or two. I guess they could have been positioning it.''

''Had there been things on the shelves?''

Shields narrowed his eyes as he clearly thought over the question. ''Yeah,'' he said finally, ''I think there might have been. I saw some broken dishes in the debris, a cup or something. Maybe a plate.'' He nodded a little more confidently. ''Yeah, I'm pretty sure it had stuff in it.''

''Where was Vicki?'' he asked quietly.

''Close to the base,'' Shields replied. ''She was probably right next to it when it fell. Kevin was about two, maybe three feet behind her.''

''On their backs or their stomachs?''

Shields frowned for a moment before answering. ''Stomachs,'' he said finally.

Grant registered the information in silence, then spoke slowly. ''She'd had the piece retrofitted with wall brackets so it'd stay up in case of an earthquake. Did you see whether or not those had been unscrewed?''

''I didn't notice,'' the fireman said. ''We had our hands full getting them out. I could call the Courage Bay Police Department and have the examiner phone you, though. I know they sent a unit to the scene so they could file a report.''

Grant shook his head. ''I appreciate the offer but I'll contact him myself a little later.''

He could feel the other man's curiosity. Grant couldn't satisfy it, though. Shields was too close to Andrea and anything Grant said would find its way back to her, he was sure.

''What else can I do?'' Shields asked.

Grant met the fireman's gaze. It seemed steady and honest and Grant had the fleeting thought that Alex Shields was just the kind of man a woman like Andrea Hunt would hook up with—good-looking, strong, a real all-American type. An unexpected pang of regret hit Grant, but he pushed it aside and shook his head. ''I think I can handle it from here.''

THE EVENING PASSED QUIETLY, Andrea on one side of Kevin's bed, Grant on the other. From time to time she looked at the man who sat in the shadows but for the most part, they each pretended the other one wasn't there. For Andrea, that wasn't an easy task.

Grant seemed to dominate the space—not because of his physical presence but because of his overwhelming intensity. She felt as if she could hear his heart beat and see his blood rushing through his veins. The reaction was weird and she told herself she was imagining things, but as the hours passed and the hospital became quieter, the feeling grew. After a while, she decided their bodies had synchronized in some strange fashion, her heart matching his rhythm, his breathing keeping time with hers.

The strident sound of the telephone brought her out of the bizarre thoughts. The unit was on Grant's side and he answered it before the first ring stopped.

Andrea's eyes went to the sleeping child in the bed. He was completely under. Nothing could have penetrated his exhaustion, or the painkillers the doctor had given him.

"Andrea?" Grant spoke her name in a whisper as he held out the phone. "It's your mother...."

She nodded and came around the bed, taking the receiver from him. "Mom?"

"I had to call and see how Kevin was," her mother said. "Is everything all right?"

"He's sound asleep," Andrea answered. "They put the cast on and brought him up after you guys left. He was too tired to do anything but zonk out."

"That's good," she said with relief in her voice.

Andrea wished she could blurt out her concerns over Kevin's future, but with Grant five feet away, she didn't dare. The discussion would have to wait until she had her parents alone.

"Are you okay?" Andrea asked instead.

"It's been tough," her mother answered. "We...

we took care of everything." She made a sound halfway between a cough and a sob. "The services will be day after tomorrow. In the afternoon." She recited the details with excruciating precision. Even though Andrea didn't want to hear about caskets and flowers and music, she let her mother talk until everything was out.

"Are you going to stay there tonight?"

Andrea glanced at Grant. He'd switched places with her and was now sitting in the chair she'd abandoned. His cheeks were dark with unshaven stubble, the circles under his eyes darker still.

"Yes, I am," Andrea said firmly. "I want to be here if Kevin wakes up and gets scared."

"Good, good… I think that's a good idea."

The Hunts were a tough bunch but Andrea could hear the strain in her mother's words. They said goodbye and Andrea hung up the phone.

GRANT WATCHED ANDREA. When he'd returned to the room after his conversation with Alex, she'd been quiet and subdued. He hadn't tried to talk to her but sooner or later, he'd need to ask her some of the same questions—and probably more—that he'd asked the fireman. If something had happened in that house other than an accident, Grant *had* to know. Until he was sure, though, he wasn't going to say a word to Andrea.

He stood and stretched, then looked down at

Kevin. He was sleeping peacefully. He caught Andrea's eye and spoke. "Is your mom all right?"

"She's tired," Andrea answered. "They went to the funeral home and made all the arrangements."

"Your parents are good people," he said. "And strong. They'll come through this just fine." Almost as an afterthought, he added, "You will, too."

She seemed surprised by his words of praise but she didn't comment.

"When are the services?"

She told him then fell mute again. The stillness between them could have been awkward, yet it didn't feel that way to Grant. It felt right. And that, in turn, seemed strange. In all their years of marriage, he and Vicki had never shared a silence like this.

He sat down again and leaned his head against the leather chair. On the other side of the room, Andrea did the same. A moment later, their eyes met over Kevin's bed.

Andrea looked away first.

CHAPTER FIVE

SHE WOKE TO THE SMELL of coffee. For half a second, Andrea thought she was back at the fire station, then she opened her eyes. Grant stood before her with a mug, steam rising from the top as he held it out. The coffee was black and hot and she drank it down, her eyes going to the bed and the small boy who still slept.

"He didn't wake all night," Grant said. "Barely moved. A couple of times, I actually got up and made sure he was still breathing." His expression immediately turned sheepish as if he'd said more than he'd intended.

"It's the painkillers," Andrea replied. "They have strange effects on kids—they either sleep like a rock or get wired."

Outside the room, the nurses were talking and laughing, the sound providing a sharp contrast to Grant's next question. "Does he know Vicki's dead?"

"I'm not sure," she said. "I didn't bring it up because I—I wasn't certain how to explain it," she confessed. "Or if I even should." She raised her eyes, her throat constricting. "How do you tell a kid his mother is gone?"

"I've done it," he said, "but it's not something I want to do again." He paused, his voice heavy with dread and the knowledge of what was to come. "He's got to know, though. One of us has to do it."

"Let me." She could tell her words surprised him. They surprised her, too, but all at once she wanted to spare Grant that horrible task. Her reaction might have had something to do with the way he looked. Sometime during the night, he'd gained a haunted look.

Being the man he was, he started to object. "That's not what I meant! I think—"

She interrupted him. "It'll be easier for Kevin if I do it. If you tell him, he'd want to be tough and not cry. This isn't the time for that."

She could see he wanted to argue but couldn't because he knew she was right.

When Kevin finally woke up, he was groggy and fussy but he calmed down as Andrea talked to him, his gaze returning continually to the corner where his father sat.

Andrea reached over and smoothed Kevin's hair after he finished his late breakfast. "Do you know where I work, Kevin?"

He shook his head.

"I'm a paramedic," she said. "I work at the fire station and ride in the ambulance. When someone gets hurt, I take care of them. It's a pretty important job." She stopped briefly as if just now considering the idea. "Maybe when you're feeling okay, I could take you down there. You could meet the firemen and see the trucks. Would you like that?"

A tiny smile broke out and he nodded again.

"All right, then," she said. "We have a date." The explanation of her job brought her momentarily back into the real world. She glanced down at her watch. It was almost noon on Wednesday, the second day of her forty-eight hours off. By now, everyone at the station knew what had happened, but protocol was protocol. She should call in. Immediately she realized she could use the opportunity to phone her mother, too. She looked down at Kevin again.

"In fact, I have to tell my boss where I am, just in case he might need me. The call might take a while so I'm going to step outside to make it. While I'm gone, you can visit with your father, how's that?"

Kevin's reaction was instantaneous. He grabbed her hand and began to scream.

GRANT JUMPED to his feet and lunged for the bed, but instead of making things better, this had Kevin shrieking louder. Within seconds, every nurse on the floor had arrived and Grant and Andrea were both pushed into the hall.

Grant turned on Andrea in fury. "What in the hell did you do to him?"

"What did *I* do to him?" She looked at him with an incredulous stare. "What did *you* do is the question."

"What did I… What are you talking about? One minute you were standing there talking to him and the next thing I know, he's screaming his head off."

"You didn't hear what I asked him?"

"No." He wasn't about to explain that his mind had been exactly where it'd been the day before—on his growing concern that Vicki's death hadn't been an accident. "I…I was thinking of something else. Something to do with…with work."

She gave him a withering stare, then repeated what she'd said to Kevin. Grant's mouth fell open and he blinked in confusion.

"Are you sure he understood you?"

"He understood completely. What's confusing about 'visit with your father'?"

Grant shook his head in disbelief. He didn't want to believe Vicki would have poisoned Kevin against him but what other conclusion could he reach?

"Why is Kevin scared of you, Grant?" Andrea asked with suspicion.

"He *isn't* scared of me, dammit! I've been in the

room with him all night long and he didn't have a problem. You saw us talking yesterday—did he look scared of me then?''

His question stopped her. ''No,'' she admitted, ''he seemed fine at that point.''

''So what's changed?''

She bit her bottom lip then released it. ''I don't know. Maybe the meds are getting to him….'' She glanced down the hall then brought her attention back to Grant, crossing her arms. ''Whatever it is, I don't think you should go back in. Not now. He needs to calm down.''

Grant started to argue, then reminded himself of what mattered—Kevin.

''You're right,'' he said, his tone defeated, his shoulders slumping. ''I've got an errand to take care of anyway. I'll handle that then come back. Maybe he'll be okay by then.''

Andrea nodded but as her eyes met his, Grant felt like he'd stepped back in time. The distrust he saw there brought to mind Vicki and all the arguments they'd had.

The feeling wasn't one he enjoyed.

THE NURSES CAME OUT and told Andrea that everything was fine. She returned to Kevin's room, shaken and disturbed. He seemed okay yet she didn't miss the fact that he looked behind her as she came toward the bed. He wanted to make sure she was alone.

She took his hand and made her voice light. ''Hey, buddy, what the heck was that all about, huh? You scared the baloney out of me!''

He blinked and turned away. She pressed him a bit more, but he was clearly exhausted, and with no other option, Andrea fell silent. He went to sleep within minutes.

She'd dealt with a lot of abused children over time and Andrea could recognize the symptoms.

They weren't here.

Whatever Kevin had reacted to, it didn't involve abuse. He'd been scared for a different reason, but what that reason might be was a complete mystery.

With Grant gone, Andrea picked up the phone next to the bed, the incident weighing heavily on her mind. She called the station and talked to her boss, the captain of Squad 1, Joe Ripani. He knew about the accident, of course, and reassured her, giving her his condolences as well. ''Take all the time you need, Andie. We understand. If something comes up, I'll call you but don't worry for now. And I'm very sorry about your sister.''

The call she made next was more difficult. When her dad answered, his voice was so hoarse she knew he'd been crying. She'd never seen him act any way but strong and in control and hearing his pain she swallowed hard, her words faltering.

"Dad...it...it's Andrea.... I need to talk to you and Mom about something."

"Oh, my God—is Kevin—"

"He's fine." She reassured him. "Just fine. It's not about him. Well, in a way, it is, but it's about him and Grant...."

Her father sighed and said, "Let me get your mother."

Andrea's mom picked up a moment later. "What's wrong, sweetheart?"

Andrea had intended only to relay Grant's plans but she found herself telling her mother about Kevin's strange reaction, the words pouring out. "I don't know what to think about it," she said finally. "Kevin seemed afraid of Grant yet not really. It's hard to explain."

"But you said Grant was sitting right there. Did Kevin scream when his dad came to the bed or before?"

"That's a good question," Andrea said slowly. "I'll have to think about it."

"You never know what kids are thinking, Andrea. Kevin was already having problems, so who knows? It's been a while since he even saw Grant. I wouldn't worry too much about it."

"You may be right," Andrea replied, "but there is one thing we do need to worry about."

"What's that?"

"Grant himself. He told me last night he doesn't

intend to leave Kevin. At all. I'm afraid he might want him when this is all over.''

A long silence echoed down the line. ''I never thought about that. I just assumed…''

''The same thing I did? That we'd take care of Kevin after this?''

''Of course.''

''I don't know, Mom. He seems pretty determined.''

''But how could he raise a child? He's single. He works all day. He's—''

''He's Kevin's father,'' Andrea interrupted. ''And the courts might agree with him if it comes to that.''

Inhaling so sharply Andrea could hear it, her mother dropped her voice and spoke softly. ''Your father is already talking about everything he wants to do with Kevin—I think it's the only thing that's keeping him going right now.'' Her next words confirmed Andrea's earlier concerns. ''I've never seen him so devastated, so…disconsolate….''

''I'm worried about him,'' Andrea confessed. ''He didn't act this way when Grandpa died.''

''I know,'' her mother replied in a low voice. ''But this is different. One day your parents pass on and you accept that sad fact, but you don't expect to…'' She hesitated, then pulled herself together, surprising Andrea once more with her strength. "You don't expect to lose a child," she finished. "That isn't the order of things."

Andrea had the thought that her mother and father were reversing the roles she'd watched them play all her life. Before now her father had been strong and able, her mother, the one who'd depended on his strength. Had they really been that way or had Andrea only seen one side of their relationship? It made her wonder.

Her mother's voice brought her back to the real problem. "If we lose that boy to Grant, Andrea, I'm afraid we'll lose your father, too."

"Then we can't let that happen," Andrea said firmly. "For Dad's sake or for Kevin's."

They hung up, and with her hand still on the phone, Andrea stared again at her sleeping nephew. Less than twenty-four hours ago, she'd been feeling sorry for herself because of her own piddling problems. The future of a child was so much more significant...

After an hour's nap, Kevin opened his eyes. He looked around then smiled at her sweetly and held out his hand. Her heart melting, Andrea grasped his fingers in hers.

She got him some juice and as he drank it, she started to worry. What had she been thinking when she'd offered to tell him his mother was gone? She didn't know how to talk to kids, much less break that kind of news.

Stepping to the window, Andrea looked down at the parking lot below, her brain churning. The sun glinted off the car tops and reflected back into her eyes. She blinked against the glare, then turned to face the child in the bed.

"Kevin, we need to talk about what happened," she started. "I know it's not something fun but it's better for us to let our feelings out. Keeping them all shut up inside can make us hurt even more. Do you understand what I'm saying?"

He looked at her without moving and she knew it was going to be worse than she thought.

Andrea went to the bed and perched on one edge, a hard lump of grief forming in her throat. She spoke around it, doing just what she'd told the child was bad—hiding her feelings.

"When the armoire fell over," she said, "your mom was standing really close to it. She was behind where you were, remember? You're the one who showed me where she was."

Not expecting an answer, she continued. "Well, after the firemen rescued you, they brought her out, too, but her injuries were a lot more serious than yours. She was hurt very badly."

His eyes reminded her of Grant's. Not quite as dark but just as reserved, his feelings well-hidden. What else made him like his daddy? Did he have a temper? Did he keep secrets? Could he read her mind? It occurred to her that she knew more than she thought she did about Grant Corbin, and that she'd learned all those things in the past twenty-four hours.

She took Kevin's fingers in hers. "She was hurt so badly, Kevin, the doctors couldn't make her well again. She died, sweetheart."

He looked at her with his sad, steady eyes.

"Do you understand what I'm saying?"

He nodded and licked his lips. For a heartbeat, it seemed as if he was going to say something. Andrea held her breath and leaned closer. "I'm very sorry," she said. "But accidents like this happen and we don't know why."

"It wasn't an accident," he said in a voice that sounded rusty. "It was all my fault."

THE SMALL HOUSE WAS PERCHED at the end of a cul-de-sac, a larger and much older home to one side of it, an empty lot on the other. Grant had been surprised when Andrea had told him Vicki had moved into the place where they'd grown up, but Vicki had always had a practical side. She'd consistently done what she needed to for her and for Kevin and a rent-free home would have appealed to her.

From the curb where he was parked, Grant studied the surrounding area. Both houses sat at the base of a cliff. They had small, almost nonexistent backyards, more generous ones out front. He turned to his right and stared out the passenger side window. The street he'd come up had been steep, but the rewards were obvious. He could see almost the entire southern end of the bay. Vicki had once come home with a sapphire ring she'd *said* she'd bought for herself. As the deep blue water shimmered in the heat, he was reminded of that expensive bauble.

That, in turn, took his thoughts down a different road. Holly had phoned him late last night and passed on the message that someone at the Courage Bay Wells Fargo Bank had called the station looking for him. Grant had stopped at the bank building on the way over where he'd learned he'd been named the trustee of an account Vicki had established for Kevin. When the banker had told Grant the fund held more than sixty thousand dollars, he'd almost passed out.

Where in the hell had Vicki gotten that kind of money?

After his initial shock had left him, Grant had begun to focus and he'd called the police chief, a man by the name of Max Zirinsky, and introduced himself. Grant hadn't really known what to expect but when Zirinsky had offered his condolences, he'd taken advantage of his assumption that Grant was grief-stricken. He'd asked as many questions as he dared, thanking the officer, then hanging up. The bottom line was what he'd assumed it would be—pending further information, Vicki's death had already been ruled accidental and the body had been released to the funeral home.

Turning back to the houses on the street, Grant studied them both. Anyone visiting either place would have had to come up the incline just as he had, by car or by foot. You might be able to rappel down the cliff, he thought, but the landing would be tricky. He was weighing the consequences of that fact when the front door of the house on the right opened to reveal an older woman with a sweater around her shoulders.

Grant muttered "Thank you" under his breath, then got out of his car. Two minutes later he was introducing himself to a woman named Pearl Moore. A minute after that they were sitting in the rockers she had on her porch, glasses of fresh lemonade leaving rings on the table between them. Beneath a halo of silver-white hair, she regarded him with open friendliness. Vicki obviously hadn't yet had a chance to denigrate him to her neighbor.

Mrs. Moore carried the conversation easily, as old people often did, eager to talk to someone who wanted, for a change, to listen to her. Even though he had to repeat himself once or twice, Grant knew immediately she was sharp—her questionable hearing no detriment to her powers of observation. She had probably been fast asleep when the armoire went over, but she would have noted any activity beforehand. He let her ramble. He knew he'd get more unexpected information that way than he ever would by asking questions.

"I always loved those girls," the elderly lady said. "Even when they were little toots and ornery as could be. I was really looking forward to playing with Kevin. He seems like a quiet little thing, but smart, you know what I mean?"

"He *is* smart," Grant replied.

"I bet it tore you up when they moved out, huh?"

Her unexpected question pulled his gaze to her face. "How do you know they moved out?" he asked. "Maybe I was the one who left them."

"How do I know?" She repeated his question then primly folded her hands in her lap. "I told you—Vicki was a toot. She wouldn't have stayed married too long to a man as nice as you."

The tightness in Grant's chest loosened just a bit. "And how do you know I'm nice?"

She made a pfft sound as if his question was too ridiculous to even answer. "I'm an excellent judge of character, young man, and I always have been. I can look at a person and tell if he cheats at cards. Or if he does worse…."

She leaned closer, putting her wrinkled elbow on the arm of her chair as she cut her gaze to Grant. "I'm not tellin' you anything I suppose you don't already know, but Vicki always liked to…run with a wild bunch. Andrea wasn't like that—she had a good head on her shoulders even when she was a kid—but Vicki…'' Her silver hair glimmered as she shook her head. ''Vicki knew how to find trouble. From the looks of things, I'd say that hadn't changed any, either.''

Grant spoke calmly. ''What do you mean?''

''She'd only been back a few hours but she'd had a steady stream of people in and out.'' She held up an arthritic hand, her knuckles large and misshapen as she folded down her fingers, one by one, and counted Vicki's visitors. ''First there was the moving van, and then the cable guy. Next came the phone man and after he left, the pizza delivery truck came! I hadn't had that many cars up here in years. The renters before her were nice people, real quiet.'' She looked at her fingers in a puzzled way, then her face cleared as she remembered the last visitor. ''There was one other car, too, but it came early, early yesterday morning. I hadn't gotten up yet. I heard the car leave, though, and I got up to take a peek.''

She stopped. ''You know…just to make sure everything was all right.''

''Of course,'' Grant answered. ''Good neighbors check on each other.''

She nodded vigorously. ''They certainly do.''

''Did you tell the Courage Bay police what you saw?''

''No sir, I did not.''

"Why?"

"They didn't ask."

Grant suppressed a smile. "That makes sense.... Did you see who was driving?"

"Well, it was still dark and I was half asleep, but I did notice a few things," she said. "It was a big car, one of those truck thingies...."

"An SUV?"

"Yes." She nodded again. "An SUV. It was black with those tinted windows, you know? I had a feeling there was only one person inside but I couldn't say for sure." She dug into the pocket of the apron she wore and pulled out a scrap of paper. It was the corner of a magazine—*Ladies Home Journal*—and as she handed it over, Grant looked up in surprise.

"I copied down the license plate number," she confirmed. "Just in case. You know...good neighbors—"

He finished the sentence for her "—check on each other."

She beamed at him then patted his hand and refilled his lemonade glass.

ANDREA STARED at Kevin, her heart in her throat. She didn't know which surprised her more, the fact that he'd actually spoken or the words he'd voiced. She said the first thing that came into her mind. "Kevin, sweetie! It *was* an accident, okay? You didn't have anything to do with what happened. Nothing at all!''

He looked at her, his lips so tightly screwed together it seemed as if he were afraid she might try and force him to speak again. Which is exactly what she wished she could do.

Desperate to communicate with the child, Andrea put her hands on his arms and held him tight. ''Kevin, please! Listen to me. You had nothing to do with that armoire falling over. It just happened. Right now, I don't know why—maybe it was overloaded in the front or maybe it shifted somehow, who knows? But it couldn't have been your fault, okay? It couldn't have been!''

He responded by turning his head away.

She tried everything she could think of, but Kevin refused to speak again. Defeated, she sat down in the chair beside the bed and watched him drift back to sleep.

His eyes fluttered beneath his lids and he groaned, his arms and legs moving as if he were running. Her heart turned over at the burden he was carrying.

Why on earth would he think he was responsible for his mother's death? Did it have anything to do with the divorce? Her confusion growing, Andrea decided a lot of things were beginning to bother her, especially Grant Corbin.

CHAPTER SIX

THE FUNERAL WAS simple and short, the church so full of floral arrangements Andrea found their scent distracting. Her attention wandered afterward, as well, at the cemetery where she focused on Grant instead of paying attention to the minister. At some point, as she stood under the white canopy, she realized what she was doing…and why.

It was far easier to stare at Grant and frown over the flowers than it was to look at the casket and know her sister's body was inside. Andrea's eyes stung and for a second, she wanted to just give in and howl. But she couldn't because once she started, she wasn't sure she'd be able to stop.

The service was over quickly and the mourners then migrated to the Hunts' house and its air-conditioned view of Courage Bay and the surrounding mountains. Soon, the home began to hum with a dozen different conversations. Everyone in town, it seemed to Andrea, had come to the services.

Her gaze flicked over the crowd once again then she turned to the patio doors. The noise was giving her a headache. Either that, or her own thoughts were, she couldn't decide which.

Out on the cedar deck, Andrea put her hands on the railing and wished she was six again and Vicki, eight. They would have been busy with their latest project—the rescue of a squirrel from a neighborhood cat or the building of a house from a discarded refrigerator carton. They'd always found plenty to do as kids, their summer breaks never long enough for all their fun. Back then, they'd been so close.... Why had she let it slip away?

There wasn't a simple answer because nothing had happened...and that was the problem. Neither of them had made the effort to maintain their bonds and they'd drifted into their own lives, each going a different direction. Holidays brought them together in Courage Bay and the occasional phone call as well, but after Vicki had married, they simply hadn't seen each other that often, even though they'd both lived in L.A. They'd become strangers, but Andrea hadn't realized that until today...and now, it was too late.

Hearing footsteps behind her, she looked over her shoulder to see Grant approach. He wore a dark suit with a shirt and tie, all of which looked brand-new. She wondered if he'd had to go out and buy something to wear to the funeral. Maybe that had been the errand he'd had to attend to the day before.

The thought took her back to Kevin. She hadn't

told Grant—or her parents—that the little boy had spoken to her yesterday. She'd tried to find a good reason to keep his vocalization a secret but she'd come up empty-handed. There *was* no good reason. She'd simply wanted to, and so she had. When the time was right, she'd reveal that he'd spoken and what he'd said. For now, though, she kept the event to herself.

Reaching her side, Grant rested his elbows on the wooden ledge and stared out to the bay in silence. In addition to buying his suit, he'd shaved and had his hair cut. He looked more like a cop. Maybe it was the sunglasses, she thought, the dark lenses covering his eyes completely. She doubted he wore them to hide his tears. According to Vicki, the only tears that had been shed in their relationship were her own…when Grant had abandoned her and Kevin.

He finally spoke, his voice husky. "Tell me what you saw when you walked into Vicki's that day. Exactly what you saw."

The question felt intrusive, his timing awkward. Andrea didn't want to talk about it, especially right now, but Grant deserved to be given more than her cursory explanation at the hospital that day. He had the same need of all who found themselves in this position. Those closest to the dead wanted specifics, as if they'd somehow feel better once they knew everything. Andrea understood and complied even though revealing the details usually had the opposite effect.

She talked for at least fifteen minutes. He had only a few questions. When she finished, he stayed quiet for a long time, then he nodded toward the house.

"You know all the people in there?"

Expecting questions about the accident, Andrea felt relief slide over her. She turned and leaned against the wooden handrail to stare through the windows. "Pretty much," she answered. "They're mostly locals, friends of Mom and Dad's."

"See anyone you don't recognize?"

"I'm sure there's got to be someone but for the most part, they're familiar." She looked at him with open curiosity. "Why are you asking?"

"Vic had a lot of friends," he said casually. "Some of the L.A. crowd might have come down. You wouldn't have known them so I wanted to introduce you."

His answer was disingenuous.

"I don't imagine they've had time to find out about her death," Andrea replied. "It happened so fast. There's a register, though. If I see an unfamiliar name I'll ask you about it later and drop them a note to thank them for coming."

He nodded and changed the subject again. "I appreciate your friend Alex visiting with Kevin this afternoon. Are you positive he didn't mind?"

"He said it wasn't a problem. He'll probably put the poor kid to sleep with all his firefighting stories."

"I bet he has plenty." Grant watched her thoughtfully. "It's a dangerous job. Do you worry about him?"

"Alex can take care of himself." Her answer came automatically then she realized what Grant had really meant. "He's not my boyfriend, if that's what you're thinking. We're just friends, that's all."

He looked at her as if that had been the last question on his mind and she instantly felt the fool. She started to compound the problem by saying more, but she managed to stop herself.

"Kevin will be all right," she said stiffly. "I'll be going back to the hospital as soon as I can."

"So will I." After a lengthy pause, he spoke again. "Did you figure out why he got so upset yesterday?"

"No," she said quickly. Too quickly.

They stared at each other in the bright sunlight. Grant stood closer to her than she would have liked. There were flecks of gray in his hair and he had a tiny round dot at the bottom of his earlobe that surprised her. He didn't seem like a guy who'd wear an earring, but he'd obviously had one at some point in his life, albeit a while back.

Her eyes gave her away.

He rubbed a finger over the spot. "I worked Vice. Wearing an earring was de rigueur."

"Vicki never mentioned that."

"It was before her time. I was undercover for almost six years. In Hollenbeck."

"Six years is quite a stretch, especially in L.A." She raised an eyebrow. "Most people can't handle it six months, much less six years."

His gaze went back to the bay and she felt him pull away from her, mentally but not physically. "I fit in well," he said darkly.

She understood his explanation. Surrounding yourself with other people's crises left little time for personal examination, a situation she'd found helpful herself. But staring at his stony profile, she suddenly wondered if that was what he'd meant. Maybe he was saying he, himself, fit into that sordid world. The thought was as unsettling as his expression.

"What division are you in now?" she asked to distract herself.

"Homicide."

"Do you like it?"

"It's a job."

A stilted silence filled the air around them, then Grant seemed to shake himself free from his thoughts.

"You like being a paramedic?" he asked.

"It's a job." She echoed his words but smiled.

"I've done it for so long I can't imagine doing anything else."

"You worked in L.A., though, didn't you? Why'd you come back here?"

"That's personal. I don't discuss it."

Without saying a word or even changing expressions, he stared at her. A second passed, or was it an hour?

She sighed. "I'm sorry. I didn't mean to be rude, but I guess I'm just a little sensitive about it, that's all."

Through the sliding glass doors that led inside, her eyes sought out her mother and father. They were standing side by side, their arms wrapped around each other, in support. Forty years they'd been married. What did that feel like?

"Heart problems," he said. "Say no more. I understand."

His perception shocked her. Andrea started to ask him what he knew about the subject—all he'd done was hurt her sister—but then she saw his eyes and stopped. They were full of pain, so raw and fresh, she found herself holding her breath.

Then she found herself telling him the truth.

"I fell in love with someone I shouldn't have," she said. "It wasn't the first time I've made that kind of mistake, but it was the first time for this reason...." She paused. "I didn't know he was married and had two kids."

Considering what she knew about Grant and his own infidelity, she couldn't believe she was revealing this to him. He made it impossible for her to lie, though.

His gaze was so sharp it could have drawn blood. "How could you not know something like that?"

"That's a damn good question," she said. "I've asked myself the very same thing a thousand times, and I still don't have an answer. I'm just an idiot, I guess."

She started to add "What's your excuse?" but before she could do so, her mother stepped to the door and motioned for Andrea to come back inside.

Andrea pushed off the railing and went back inside. Grant's response—if he had one—went unheard.

GRANT LEFT the Hunts' house an hour later. The curious looks were getting to him, but more importantly, he wanted to think about what Andrea had told him. After visiting with Mrs. Moore last night, Grant had driven off, then doubled back. He'd searched Vicki's place and had found exactly what he'd expected to find: no attempt whatsoever had been made to install the armoire's earthquake protection equipment. Grant headed toward the hospital to see his son and think about what that meant.

In the meantime, he worried over Kevin's reaction the day before. He wanted to question the child, but Grant knew he'd never hear the truth with Andrea near. To find out anything he had to talk to Kevin alone.

Of course, Andrea hadn't wanted him to leave. She'd known he would head straight for the hospital. Unable to do the same without abandoning her parents, she'd had to stay put, but her conflict had been clear. She couldn't keep secrets.

Not even about herself.

Grant had been surprised by her unexpected revelation. Andrea Hunt was the last person he would have thought capable of falling for a married man. It must be something in the sisters' genes, he decided. Some kind of inherited predisposition to infidelity. He pushed the thought from his head and pulled into a shopping center he'd spotted the day before. Completing his errand in record time, he continued to the hospital, but before he could park, his beeper sounded. Glancing at the numbers, he hurried inside to the bank of phones by the reception desk. He'd called Parker last night and passed on all the information Mrs. Moore had given him. He must have found out something if he was calling back this soon.

"What do you have?" Grant asked tersely.

"Not much," his partner replied. "The plates are registered to a private corporation. I'm trying to track down the principals but it may take a while. The situation's getting a little complicated."

Grant wasn't surprised. If the vehicle Mrs. Moore had spotted belonged to who he'd initially suspected, it'd take Park a while to get those names, if ever. The people behind this one were experts at burying information. And other things, too.

Park lowered his already deep voice. "I'm catching some heat, Grant."

"From who?"

"The captain. He bitched like an old lady about my report on the Davila case, but there's nothing wrong with it. Something tells me he just wanted to give me some grief. Said I needed to reinterview all the wits and do some other crap like that. Busy-work. Someone up the ladder ain't happy."

"Well, I appreciate the help, Park. Watch your back, okay?"

"No problem, man. We'll be in touch."

They hung up, and Grant headed down the hallway to the nearest set of elevators. As he rose to the fourth floor, he decided he didn't like the way this was going.

Kevin grinned when Grant entered his room a few minutes later and a fifty-ton weight fell from Grant's shoulders. Whatever had frightened Kevin yesterday had obviously been temporary. Maybe it'd even been the drugs, as Andrea had suggested.

Grant thanked Alex Shields and watched the fireman depart, then he turned his attention to Kevin and handed over the sack from the toy store where he'd stopped.

Kevin tore into the bag with delight. His jaw dropped and Grant lip-read the "Wow" that he mouthed. The present was expensive and extravagant but Grant didn't care. He had the game box attached to the room's television within minutes and two seconds after that, Kevin was happily shooting at monsters, the sound effects as startling as the creatures who died a thousand deaths.

Grant let him play for some time, then he brought up the subject he had to discuss before Andrea returned.

"Let's take a break," he suggested, sitting down on the bed. "And talk just a bit."

Kevin's mouth turned down with disappointment, but he put away the controls and looked at Grant expectantly.

"I want to know what upset you yesterday," Grant said. "You almost seemed like you were scared of me. I'd hate to think that's the case."

Kevin blinked.

"*Are* you scared of me?"

He pursed his mouth, then shook his head.

"That's good," Grant answered with relief. "It'd really bother me if I'd done something that frightened you. I love you, Kevin, and I always have. You know that, don't you?"

Kevin dropped his gaze to the blanket that covered his bed and picked at it with nervous fingers.

Grant spoke softly. "No one told you otherwise, did they? Because if they did, they would have been wrong. Maybe they were confused or upset or not thinking too straight, but I love you, Kev, and that will never change."

His fingers stilled, then the little boy looked up. His brown eyes were wet but he blinked rapidly, refusing to let the tears fall.

"I love you," Grant repeated. "And I hope you love me, too."

Kevin nodded again, then threw his arms around Grant's neck and held on tightly. Grant closed his eyes and returned the hug, his throat swelling with unexpected emotion.

They both recovered, then Kevin resumed his seemingly endless fascination with the destruction of various aliens. He was still hard at it when the doctor entered.

After he finished his examination, the physician looked at Grant and smiled. "I think your boy's going to be fine. His ankle is already stronger. I wish all my patients healed so quickly." They chatted for a bit more, then the doctor tapped Kevin's chart against the end of his bed.

"Are you ready to go home, young man?"

Kevin nodded emphatically.

"I'll probably release you fairly soon, then."

The doctor turned to Grant. "Someone will stop by later to advise you about his physical therapy. We won't keep that cast on long. After it's off, he'll need a few weeks, maybe a month's worth of PT." He looked at Kevin. "You'll be in fine shape real soon, I promise." He saluted the little boy in the bed and left.

Kevin resumed his game as Grant thought about this new complication. He'd never considered the possibility of physical therapy. How was he going to handle that?

Grant didn't mention the new problem when Jack and Karen Hunt came an hour later. Andrea's parents were clearly exhausted by the ordeal of the funeral, but Jack Hunt seemed to find new energy as he hugged his grandson and exclaimed over his new toy. Kevin seemed equally pleased to see his grandparents. Grant took in the transformations and tried to convince himself it wasn't significant.

Karen Hunt watched her husband and grandson for a while. Then she caught Grant's eye. "I'm sure you must be tired, Grant. Why don't we stay and visit with Kevin and you can make an early night of it?"

Grant didn't want to leave Kevin alone but sooner or later, he was going to have to do just that. Still he hesitated.

Jack Hunt looked up. "We need some time with him, Grant."

The simple truth reached Grant as nothing else might have. Need was something he understood all too well.

"Of course," he said. "I could use the rest, sure." Telling Kevin to be good, he shook hands with the older man, kissed Karen lightly then stepped from the room.

Feeling restless and edgy, he went downstairs. Even though night had fallen several hours before, the Impala was an oven when he opened the door. Releasing the hot air that had been trapped inside, Grant rolled down all the windows then started the car but before he put it in gear, he paused to think. When he pulled out of the parking lot, he turned left—toward Vicki's house—instead of right, toward his hotel.

Sleep could wait, his questions couldn't.

ANDREA OPENED the front door of her childhood home with the keys her mother had given her. Standing in the stifling darkness, she stared at the debris still scattered around the living room. The sight made her head spin and the same feeling of wrongness she'd felt on Tuesday hit her again, this time even stronger. Her throat went tight as she dismissed the reaction. She *knew* what was wrong now—her sister was dead. And if Andrea didn't take care of things, her nephew might be lost to her as well.

The thought put her feet into motion and she refocused on the reason she'd come by—to pick up some toys for Kevin as a surprise. Grant was probably filling Kevin's head right now with wonderful stories about the two of them living together. If it came down to a fight for the little boy's affection, Andrea was more than prepared to battle Grant with anything she had at her disposal, but she was very much aware of her status. She was only the aunt. Being Kevin's father gave Grant a built-in advantage.

She headed for the bedrooms without bothering to turn on the lights. She'd walked the path a thousand times, the dim street lamp outside, along with her memory, providing more illumination than she needed.

The first bedroom on the left had been Vicki's room when they were children. At the doorway, Andrea stopped, guessing, correctly, that Vicki would put her own son here. A half-dozen open boxes were spread around the room, some partially unpacked, others still full. Kevin had removed a few clothes, but it was clear which one was most important to him—the one that held his toys. She bent down to pick up the nearest plush animal, a small black cat. Its right ear was torn and the stuffing was dribbling out, a sure sign of its favored status, she decided. She tucked it into her purse, then selected a few more things from those scattered on his bed.

She returned to the hall and started toward the living room, but halfway there, she turned, her curiosity getting the better of her. Heading for the bedroom that had once been her own, Andrea automatically ran her fingers against the wall, just as she had as a kid. When she came to the small closet that housed the hot water heater, she wasn't surprised to see the door ajar. The old house had its quirks and they hadn't changed...the latch had always been loose. She pushed the door shut without thinking, then went inside her old room.

The space was empty except for a few boxes and a small computer desk and chair. There were books and papers flung about, a box of files and computer disks on the floor. It'd always seemed odd to Andrea, but her scatterbrained sister had been a bookkeeper. Generally working for smaller businesses that didn't need the services of a full C.P.A., she'd maintained their accounts from home. She'd obviously been going to use this room as an office. Andrea looked at the back wall, half expecting to see the Trent Reznor and Nine Inch Nails poster she'd kept there when she'd been sixteen. A framed political placard for a state senator she'd never heard of was hanging in its place instead. Andrea studied it briefly then dismissed the garish graphics and airbrushed photos. Vicki had always had a weird sense of art—even as a kid she'd decorated with strange photos and ads she'd cut out of magazines. She'd probably found this at a garage sale and bought it on a whim, liking the color or the composition for some bizarre reason only she would understand.

Returning to the hall, Andrea glanced inside the master bedroom but didn't go in. Vicki had left a greater mess than her son, her clothes thrown on the bed, boxes overturned, their contents strewn about. The room looked as if the proverbial tornado had hit and Andrea had to shake her head. Vicki had never been one for order, that was sure.

Andrea left, her earlier impatience returning. As she reached the end of the hall, however, she found herself going right, into the kitchen, where a faint light glowed. The oven lamp had been left on. Andrea flipped the switch then walked into the dining room, her steps quickening as she went back to the front door.

But all at once she stopped.

Something wasn't right. Staring at the boxes, Andrea frowned, unable to pinpoint exactly what bothered her. The realization took a moment, but when it came, it rippled down her spine with a coldness that took away her breath.

The boxes *had* been lined against the wall, next to the windows, and all of them had been closed. That was no longer the case. More than one or two were open. Some of their contents, along with the packing material, had been removed and plates and dishes now covered the polished mahogany table.

Bathed in darkness, Andrea gripped the back of the nearest chair, her breathing suddenly loud and harsh in the silence.

Clearly, someone had been inside the house, but who? And why?

Andrea tried to remember if the front door had been locked when she inserted the key but her brain wouldn't cooperate. Instead, it was busy listening for noises she might have missed and staring into the corners for objects obscured by the shadows. Her heart began to race.

She told herself that whoever had been here wasn't here now. She'd been through the entire place and if anyone had been hiding, she would have found him.

But she hadn't gone into the bathrooms. Or the garage. Or the back porch…

She was being ridiculous. She was alone. No one else was in the house. And even if that weren't the case, she was a big girl. She could take care of herself and had done so on many different occasions. Paramedics *had* to have that skill.

But this was different, a little voice answered. *This was very different. And you knew it when you first came inside, remember? You sensed it.*

She hushed the voice and started forward. She'd read in the paper once about thieves who checked funeral notices then broke into the bereaved's homes while everyone was gone. Maybe that was what had happened here.

Skirting the table, she hurried back into the living room and flipped on the lights. Nothing moved or jumped out at her. With grim determination she put down her purse then went back through the house, this time, going into every room. She ended up at the back door, rattling the knob to make sure it was still locked, the knowledge that she was truly alone somehow less comforting than she expected. Dousing the lights, she left by the front door, latching it firmly behind her.

She was halfway down the sidewalk when she heard footsteps behind her.

CHAPTER SEVEN

As GRANT'S HAND CLOSED around Andrea's elbow, she dropped her purse and pivoted. The abruptness of her movement tipped him off...but just barely. He raised his left hand at the very last second and captured her right fist an inch from his face.

He clamped his fingers around hers and held them fast. They stood so close they could have been mistaken for lovers except for the look on Andrea's face. It was fearful.

"What the hell are you doing?" he demanded. "You damn near clipped me."

Her expression changed to anger. She was breathing hard, and her breasts brushed against his arm as she spoke. "I was walking down the side-walk, minding my own business! Why'd you go after me like that?"

Grant opened his fist and released her hand. "You're the one who swung first. I was only trying to get your attention...."

"Well, do it another way next time." She dusted

her fingers over her right knuckles as if he'd somehow marked her. "You scared me."

"What's going on, Andrea? Why are you so uptight?"

"I am not uptight." She bent down to pick up the scattered contents of her purse. He kneeled beside her and recovered a hairbrush and three tubes of lipstick. Why on earth did she need three tubes of lipstick? Her lips were bare right now and he couldn't imagine them looking any better.

The unexpected thought went through him like a ricocheting bullet, leaving behind a trail of disbelief. What in the hell was he thinking? This was his ex-sister-in-law, for God's sake.

She grabbed her things from his hand and stood. He did as well, pulling himself together and dismissing the thoughts he shouldn't be having.

"You *are* uptight," he disputed. "And you were scared before I touched you, otherwise you wouldn't have swung at me."

She looked away and didn't answer.

"What is it?" he persisted. "You might as well tell me now because I'll keep asking until you answer."

She took a moment, then tilted her head to the house behind them, speaking reluctantly. "Someone's been inside."

Grant's first thought was that she meant him, that

she'd somehow found out he'd been there the other night and now she wanted to know why.

When he realized what she really meant, his second thought was about the money in Vicki's bank account. Did someone want it back?

On reflex, he slipped his hand inside his jacket, remembering too late he'd left his weapon locked in his car.

She saw his movement and shook her head. "They're long gone. I checked."

"That wasn't a smart thing to do."

"You're probably right," she conceded, surprising him. "But I can take care of myself."

"That's obvious." He rubbed his chin. "If I'd been a second slower, I'd be wearing a real bruise tomorrow."

She didn't answer, because she wasn't listening. Instead, she was thinking, looking over his shoulder toward the house. Her eyes narrowed almost imperceptibly then came back to Grant's face. Anyone but him might have missed the expression but he not only saw it, he knew what it meant.

She was doing exactly what he'd first feared. She was asking herself if *he* had been the one inside, going through her sister's possessions, looking for something, taking God knew what. All at once, he wondered if she knew about the money. Probably not, he decided, or she would have said something about it.

"Why aren't you at the hospital?" she asked slowly.

Too savvy to ask him outright if he'd been inside, Andrea skirted the issue. He found himself giving her credit, even though he was the one she was trying to scam.

He answered her casually. "Your parents came by and wanted to spend time with Kevin. I left them there and came here." He paused. "I wanted to see where Vicki had lived."

Just as he'd expected, her expression softened slightly. He felt like a bastard for manipulating her, but it didn't stop him.

"Would you mind?"

"Of course not," she replied. "Let's go inside right now."

They turned together and went up the steps, Grant unlocking the door with the key Andrea handed him. He held out his hand but when she preceded him, he regretted the gentlemanly gesture. Her perfume, a scent so light he almost missed it, followed in her wake. Vicki had always worn something spicy and heavy. When he'd complained she'd told him if he were more "sophisticated" he'd appreciate it. Her explanation had left little doubt in his mind where she'd gotten the fragrance.

He followed Andrea inside, adjusting his response to reflect the shock he'd actually felt the first time he'd seen the shattered armoire and imagined it falling. His performance wasn't Academy Award calibre, but Andrea seemed to buy it.

Speaking over her shoulder, she walked into the dining room then stopped. ''Those boxes weren't open,'' she said, pointing to the back of the room. ''They were lined up against that wall over there and everything was taped shut.''

He didn't give any reaction this time. ''Are you sure?'' he asked reflexively.

''Of course, I'm sure. Why would I tell you this and not be—''

He held up his hand. ''It was an automatic question, okay? Was the door locked when you got here?''

''I can't remember,'' she said, shaking her head. ''I know I used my key and came in but I wasn't really thinking about what I was doing. But the back door was fastened. I checked.''

''What about the other rooms? Same thing there?''

''I don't know…. I didn't go back there Tuesday. The rooms are all messy now, but I just assumed Vicki had left them that way.''

She walked into the kitchen to cut through to the hallway, stopping to point to the oven. ''The light was on in there. I turned it off and that's when I saw the open boxes in the dining room.'' She looked at him, her forehead furrowing. ''I don't think the light was on that morning, but I could have missed it. Why would a thief turn on the oven light, though? That doesn't make any sense…."

He said "No, it doesn't," but he thought, *Oh, shit…* Vicki had rarely cooked when they'd been married. He'd teased her once about it, saying they should hide their valuables in the oven because it was never used. She'd looked at him so strangely, the moment had stuck in his mind. Had she taken him seriously?

They continued to the rear of the home. Pausing to glance into the first two bedrooms, Grant didn't have to fake his dismay. He couldn't very well tell Andrea the rooms *hadn't* been like this before now or she'd realize he'd been in the house earlier. A sense of deep disquiet came over him.

He walked inside the last room, then flipped on the lamp beside the bed. A soft pink light replaced the darkness. Vicki had always liked to have special bulbs in their bedroom and he closed his eyes and let himself remember why.

Andrea's voice pulled him back. "Do you miss her?"

He opened his eyes and realized he'd picked up one of the nightgowns that had been lying on the bed. He spread his fingers apart and let the silk glide through them.

"No," he said. "I'm sorry she died, but I don't miss your sister." He lifted his gaze. "She wasn't an easy person to live with."

"I know."

"No, you don't," he answered. "Not like I know."

"I can guess."

"No, you can't."

Holding Andrea's stare, he moved away from the bed and came to her side. The rose-colored rays caressed her face as he tucked a loose strand of hair behind her ear.

"You can't possibly know," he repeated, "but maybe that's for the best. We shouldn't know everything about someone else. It's not a good idea. Secrets are secrets for a reason."

She stood as still as the heated air that surrounded them. "Did my sister know your secrets?"

"No." He shook his head. "I keep mine buried way too deep."

"I thought husbands and wives shared everything."

"You've never been married." It wasn't a question.

"That's true," she said. "I've been in long-term relationships before, but—"

"Was the married guy one?"

Her lips tightened. "No, he wasn't. That was a short term mistake."

"Then consider yourself lucky." Grant heard the bitterness in his voice but he didn't bother to hide it. "As time passes, things only get more complicated."

She was taller than Vicki and she could look him straight in the eye, which she did with a sudden intensity. "I guess you'd know all about that, wouldn't you?"

Grant didn't know what to make of her words or of the fact that he found himself holding her arm. Her skin was soft and tender, the coiled muscles beneath smooth and strong. "What the hell does that mean?" he asked tightly.

"You know exactly what it means." She looked down at his fingers then brought her eyes back to his. "Vicki didn't hold back, Grant. She told me everything."

"I doubt that—"

"Go ahead and doubt all you like." She plucked his fingers from her arm, dropping them as if they burned her. "It won't change a thing. I *know* the truth. Vicki told me everything," she repeated, "And my sister didn't lie."

ANDREA WAS STILL SHAKY when she got back to her place. Angry at Grant for reasons she didn't want to examine and upset by what she'd uncovered at Vicki's, she'd hoped to calm herself by stopping at the hospital to see Kevin and take him his toys. Her parents were still there though, and their demeanor was so much lighter than it had been after the funeral, she didn't want to tell them about the apparent break-in.

Or the conversation she'd had with Grant.

She'd left them alone with their grandson and had come home. Kicking off her heels, she went into the kitchen and poured a glass of milk, acknowledging to herself that more than her parents' state of mind had kept her silent. The first one was Grant. The second one was Vicki.

Her sister had said Grant had cheated on her. But Grant didn't strike Andrea as the kind of guy who would treat his marriage vows casually. He was way too intense.

Vicki had also said his girlfriend had been another cop. Getting involved with people you worked with could turn out really bad. It put your heart *and* your career in jeopardy. Grant wasn't stupid.

Finally, Vicki had said he wasn't a good father, but his devotion to Kevin was unmistakable. Despite almost wishing it was otherwise, Andrea couldn't ignore how much he loved his son. When Kevin had gotten scared, Andrea had been upset but the more she thought about it, the more she decided he must have been having a reaction to his painkillers. She'd seen the same thing happen to other children and elderly patients, as well. Kevin was obviously a very sensitive child. Believing he was responsible for the accident and his mutism both reinforced that fact.

Vicki had stretched the truth on occasion, but she had never out-and-out lied to Andrea. So was the Grant Corbin Andrea now knew totally different from the one her sister had been married to? If he was, why the change?

Andrea walked into her tiny living room and sat down, sipping her milk. The windows were open wide but the night air felt expectant and hot.

Grant *had* to have known what she meant when she'd asked him about his infidelity. He *had* to. But he'd pretended otherwise, questioning her instead. In a way, she could understand his reluctance to be honest. If Kevin's custody ended up in a courtroom, no judge would award the little boy to a man who'd abandoned him before. At least, that's what Andrea hoped.

She took another sip of milk then set the glass on her coffee table and leaned back against the sofa with a sigh. She was exhausted. The whole day had been rough. Andrea closed her eyes and thought about how she'd almost hit Grant.

Then she thought of everything else.

Like how close to her he'd stood and how his hand had felt when he'd tightened it around her fingers. She also thought about the quiet way he moved and how he filled out the shoulders of his suit. And how his eyes had seemed to peel back layers of not just her clothes, but her skin itself. And she'd even helped him, for God's sake! She'd gone and told him about that weasel, Brian. How stupid was that?

Andrea moaned, then fell sideways on the couch. She was still chastising herself when she fell asleep a few minutes later.

GRANT HAD WATCHED Andrea pull away from the curb, then he'd put his car in gear and followed her. When she'd gone south, into town, he'd headed the opposite direction. Backtracking on side roads, he returned to the house and parked at the bottom of the street, hiking the rest of the way. He didn't want the sharp-eyed Mrs. Moore to see him.

The break-in hadn't surprised him, in fact, he'd almost been waiting for it. What upset him was the fact that it'd happened and he hadn't been here. They'd probably come during the funeral, he realized, letting himself in through the back door with his credit card just as he had before. That's when he would have done it.

For a moment, he let himself consider the possibility that vandals had been in the house, but he dismissed the idea quickly. He'd found jewelry and cash in Vicki's purse—ordinary thieves wouldn't have left those behind.

He went immediately to the oven and opened it, bending down to look inside. It was empty, of course, but he ran his hand over the walls and along the wire shelves just to reassure himself. He even removed the tiny lightbulb and felt inside the cavity. If Vicki had hidden anything here, money or otherwise, it was gone now. He stood up and looked around the kitchen. When he'd previously searched the place, he hadn't had enough time to do it properly. There were hundreds of hiding places in the old house. He didn't even know what she might have had—if anything—that someone else would want.

Not that it mattered, one way or the other. The fact that someone had cared enough to break in told him all he needed to know.

He took off his jacket and flipped on the small flashlight he'd brought along. Starting at one end of the room, he worked slowly through the cabinets and drawers. For the most part, they were empty and the job went fast.

But his brain seemed stuck. As he patted down the shelves and felt through the storage areas, he kept thinking about Andrea. He thought about her perfume. He thought about her mouth. He thought about her long, long legs.

Telling himself, *again,* that he was treading dangerous ground, Grant chose to let the images run wild inside his head. At some point, he decided, he'd get tired and would shut it down.

By the time he got to Vicki's bedroom, he realized his mistake. Giving in to his urges to think about Andrea only strengthened them. Now his thoughts were more powerful than ever. Standing before him with the light softly bathing her, she'd seemed the very distillation of seduction. Forbidden yet promising. Mysterious yet innocent. Sexual in so many ways.

In fact, he realized abruptly, she'd looked exactly like her sister.

The thought was an unexpected bucket of cold water, and Grant pulled in his breath with an audible intake. What in the hell would it take for him to learn his lesson?

Vicki had used her sexuality like a weapon. She'd threatened Grant with it and cajoled him as well, getting just about anything she'd wanted. As he'd come to know her better, he'd begun to suspect that she might have been an even bigger victim than him. Sometimes she'd seemed incapable of stopping herself; her ambitions had driven her.

He looked down at the rumpled bed and wondered if those very ambitions could be the reason she'd died.

Then he wondered if Andrea shared them.

ANDREA WOKE UP tired, stiff and grateful. If her boss had less understanding, she'd be in trouble, but Joe Ripani had repeated his offer yesterday at her parents' house, telling her to take another few days off. They were well covered, he'd said with a sympathetic look. Don't come back until you're ready.

She stretched her creaking back and crawled off the sofa, the black silk skirt and blouse she'd worn to the services yesterday a total mess. Peeling them off as she walked toward the bathroom, Andrea tried to focus.

It seemed like a monumental task. Her mother and father had told her late last night that Kevin was going to be released shortly. Where would he go? And what about his therapy? Then there was Vicki's house. Andrea should handle the cleanup as soon as possible, but despite Joe's generosity, she needed to return to work, too. It wasn't fair to the team to be gone too long. Stepping under the shower, she reached for her shampoo and told herself, "one thing at a time," but the cliché had a hollow ring to it. Everything was equally important and everything needed to be handled. Now. Not later.

In an hour she was dressed and at the hospital. Much to her surprise, Kevin met her at the elevator as the doors opened to his floor. Andrea put a hand to her chest in mock shock as she took in his lightweight crutches and the huge grin on his face. "Oh, my goodness! Look at you, on your feet and everything...I can't believe it!"

He walked in a wide circle then took off awkwardly, maneuvering down the hallway, dodging med carts and nurses. A young woman came up as Andrea clapped her hands in approval.

"He's doing great," she said. "The break wasn't that bad but with everything else he went through, I wasn't sure how this was going to turn out."

A crisply dressed black woman, she had friendly eyes and a engaging manner. Sticking her hand out, she said, "I'm Quita Johnson from the physical therapy department."

Andrea took her hand. "I'm amazed. I thought it'd take much longer for him to get on his feet."

"Kids heal fast," the therapist replied. "But he will have to continue his workouts. I talked to his father about that this morning."

Andrea stiffened. The conversation she and Grant had shared yesterday evening hadn't left her mind. She found it hard to believe her sister could have lied to her about something as important as her marriage.

"Is Mr. Corbin still here?"

"I believe he is." The therapist arched her neck and looked down the corridor that led to Kevin's room. "The phone rang just as I left with Kevin and he answered it." She looked down the hall, then said, "I'd better go check on Kevin. See you later…"

Grant was still talking when Andrea opened the door to Kevin's room. An invisible barricade rose between them as he looked up and saw her, his eyes going hard, his face closing. He finished his call, clearly uncomfortable with her hearing the details of his conversation. Cops were like that, she reminded herself. The blue club was an exclusive one and they kept to themselves.

He hung up and stood. "Kevin's walking. He's on crutches but he's up."

"I saw him when I came off the elevator."

They stared at each other over the little boy's bed, his uncertain future hanging between them. Despite her earlier thoughts about which problem to tackle first, Andrea knew Kevin's situation took priority over everything.

"I've been trying to decide what to do." Walking around the end of the bed, he spoke as if he'd read her mind. "About Kevin, I mean…"

Andrea tensed. "There's nothing to decide, as far as I'm concerned. My parents and I can take care of him—"

"I'm his father. He belongs with me."

She started to protest but Grant raised his hand and touched a finger to her lips, silencing her immediately. "Let me finish…" he said softly, "then you can have your say."

He took his finger away. The touch was too brief to have had an impact, but it did anyway. She rocked back then held herself steady.

"He belongs with me," Grant repeated, holding her eyes with his. "But I love Kevin and I have to do what's best for him. Right now, what's best for him *is* to stay here, in Courage Bay.''

Andrea let out her breath in a rush.

''I can't get him back and forth to physical therapy.'' His voice was edged with anger and regret. ''I can't get him three home-cooked meals or clean clothes or friends over to play with—not at this point. I called your parents and they agreed.'' He looked out the window of the hospital room, his jaw shifting slightly before he faced her once more. ''I love him, but that's not enough right now.''

She couldn't believe her ears. It couldn't be this easy.

''He's going to stay with your mother and father while he does his physical therapy. I've arranged for him to see a counselor, too, so we can deal with his not talking. Your parents' stability will be good for him and having him around will help them, too. It's a temporary setup,'' he warned. ''I intend to make the necessary arrangements to raise him myself but for the time being, I've decided this would be best.''

Andrea sat down on the bed and looked up at Grant. She wanted to trust him but Vicki's voice wouldn't let her. *He's dumping his responsibilities again. He's walking away because he doesn't care and he never has.*

''Why are you doing this?'' Andrea asked.

His eyes went dark. "I told you why. It's what's best for Kevin."

"But what about you?"

"What about me?" he asked.

"I thought you loved him. Don't you want—"

"I want him more than you'll ever understand but he's been yanked from one place to another for way too long. The poor kid doesn't know which end is up. It's time—way *past* time—that Kevin had someone put him first."

The implication was obvious.

"I believe my sister did that." Andrea's voice was firmer than she felt.

"She didn't," he countered. "She decided what she wanted to do, then she did it. Kevin's needs were never her first priority. Her own desires held that place."

Andrea jumped up. The movement put her closer to Grant but she didn't care. Her ire rose with her. "How can you say that? You're the one who abandoned them!"

"We've been over this before," he said with more than a hint of heat. "You didn't believe me then and you obviously haven't changed your mind, but I'll say it one more time: Your sister did not tell you the full story."

"Then why don't you tell me?" she demanded. "All you've done is dispute what she said. If you want me to know what you think is the truth, then spit it out.''

Grant's size made him intimidating, his deep voice only adding to the impression. ''I don't have to tell you anything and you might want to keep that in mind.''

The urge to back down was strong but Andrea fought it. ''The only facts I have to keep in mind are the ones my sister told me. You had an affair with a cop you worked with, a redhead, and you left Vicki and Kevin for her. You deserted them. That's why Vicki came back to Courage Bay. She couldn't make it in L.A. on her own so she came back here.''

Andrea drew a deep breath, her fists at her side. ''You can't waltz in here and act like the wounded widower and take that child away after his therapy is done. You don't deserve Kevin and I won't let you get him.''

They glared at each other, the inches that separated them not large enough to shield Andrea from the hot anger in Grant's eyes.

''You can't stop me,'' he said from behind clenched teeth. ''I am Kevin's father and I will decide what happens to him now. Not you. Not your parents. Take the time with him I'm giving you and be satisfied because that's all you're getting, whether you like it or not.''

CHAPTER EIGHT

HE FOUND KEVIN and kissed him goodbye, then Grant stormed out of the hospital. He'd thought long and hard about his decision to let Kevin stay with the Hunts while he completed his therapy but Andrea's reaction made Grant want to reconsider the idea.

Crossing the parking lot under the burning sun, though, Grant knew if he reneged on his promise, Kevin would be the one who paid. Grant couldn't do that to his son, or, for that matter, to Karen and Jack, who needed the boy as much as he needed them. They were good people and they didn't deserve any more grief.

Climbing into his furnace of a car, Grant was hit once more by Andrea's question. *If you want me to know what you think is the truth, then spit it out.*

Why in the hell didn't he just do that? Why didn't he tell her what kind of woman Vic had really been? He could explain the affairs and the one-night stands, the lying and the drugs. The money that had to be coming from blackmail.

He put his hands on the scorching steering wheel and answered himself.

He didn't tell Andrea because he *couldn't*.

She'd find out the truth about him as well and that would lead to his losing Kevin for sure.

Grant drove to the motel where he'd been staying and went straight to the phone. When Andrea had arrived in Kevin's room, he'd had to end off his conversation in midpoint. Sitting down on the bed, he dialed Holly Hitchen's number from memory, Andrea's voice in his ear again.

You had an affair with a cop you worked with, a redhead, and you left Vicki and Kevin for her. You deserted them.

Every lie Vicki had ever told had always contained a kernel of truth. Yeah, he'd had an affair with Holly and yeah, she was a redhead and a cop. Their relationship had ended before Vicki's time, though. Desertion had definitely taken place, too, but not the way Andrea thought.

Holly answered on the third ring. "Hitchens."

"It's me," Grant said. "Can we finish our discussion?"

Holly dismissed someone who'd been in her office then she spoke to him. "It *is* finished, as far as I'm concerned. I told you all I know. Park gave me the license plate number and the address of the organization, but when I looked them up all I got was a dead end. M.D. Ltd. is a blind trust—the assets are hidden and they're managed by a bank down in the Caymans. This has to be a front-end organization that serves as a cover for another group, but I haven't figured out who yet. Finding who actually owns that SUV your little old lady saw would take more juice than you or I could ever dream of having.''

Grant cursed softly. When the heat had gotten to Parker and he'd handed off Grant's problem to Holly, Grant had thought she'd be able to figure out what was going on. She was a bulldog when it came to details.

''What's the name of the bank?''

''Cayman State. A Hewitt Belworth is listed as the trustee, according to the records here.''

Grant scribbled the name on the back of the Courage Bay phone directory.

''Of course, even if we found out who the owners really are,'' she mused, ''it still wouldn't tell us who was driving the SUV that night.''

''I know that, Holly, but dammit—''

''Hey, I'm just the messenger,'' she shot back with equal rudeness. ''Don't take it out on me!''

Grant closed his eyes and rubbed them, weary frustration washing over him. ''You're right, you're right…. I'm sorry. I'm just trying to figure out what the hell happened down here, that's all. I guess it's getting to me.''

There was silence for a moment, then she spoke

again, her voice going husky. ''You want me there, Grant? I don't mind and I have some time off coming....''

The temptation to say yes was strong, a fantasy quickly building. As soon as the images materialized, however, Grant sent them packing—it wasn't Holly's body that he'd visualized lying beneath him.

It was Andrea's.

''I appreciate the offer, Holly, but now might not be the best time for that, if you know what I mean?''

''I understand,'' she said, her voice returning to its usual hardness. ''Let me know if I can do anything else.'' A click sounded in his ear a second later.

Grant hung up and cursed. He was in trouble too deep to measure.

KEVIN WAS RELEASED on Monday. Over the phone the evening before, Andrea and Grant had arranged to meet at the hospital. Once there, Grant was going to take care of the paperwork and then Andrea would drive the little boy to her parents. Their conversation had been stiff and awkward, Andrea still upset over the words they'd exchanged at the hospital Saturday morning.

She couldn't wait to see Grant leave. His presence was beginning to disturb her deeply, the reason for that too tangled to unravel. Over the weekend, she'd forced herself to admit that her strong reactions to him were there to stay but if he went back to L.A, maybe she'd have a chance at getting a grip on her emotions. She didn't want to battle Grant.

She didn't want to be attracted to him, either.

When she pulled up outside the hospital, he was waiting beside his son, the two of them on a bench near the circular drive.

Kevin appeared tired, the ordeal of ending his hospital stay a clear drain on his already small well of energy. Grant looked exhausted, too, but the worry on his face went further and seemed darker. The push and pull of Andrea's senses felt strange, to say the least. She left her Jeep running and came to where they sat.

She focused on Kevin. "Ready to go?"

"We're all set," Grant answered. "I explained everything and Kevin's okay with the arrangements." Grant smiled at the little boy and despite his weariness, Kevin's eyes lit up as he met his father's gaze. Andrea's heart flipped in confusion. They clearly shared a bond, a very special bond, and the proof of that was before her.

Andrea pushed aside her concerns and she and Grant loaded Kevin into her vehicle. She told herself to turn away as Grant started to say goodbye to Kevin, but she couldn't.

He took the child in his arms and said, "I want you to be really good for Grandpa and Grandma, okay? Remember what we talked about, too. They're as sad as you are about your mom so the three of you have your work cut out. I expect you to do your best."

Kevin nodded, his expression serious but determined.

Grant hugged the little boy again then he released him. "I'll be by to get you tomorrow. Don't forget we have a date now, okay? Be good." He shut the door then waved to Kevin through the window.

All at once, Andrea was glad she'd left the engine on—Kevin would be unable to hear her incredulous voice.

"I thought you were going back to L.A.," she said. "What do you mean, you 'have a date'?"

Grant looked at her, his eyes hooded. "What gave you the impression I was leaving?"

"You did. You said you were letting Kevin stay with Mom and Dad because you couldn't take care of him so…"

Standing beside the fender of her car, Grant pulled his sunglasses from his pocket and put them on. "I'm at a motel on the edge of town. It's not the kind of place a kid should be and I told your parents that. They understood. I *didn't* say I was leaving."

"But—"

"I'm sorry you misunderstood. I intend to stay here for a while, Andrea."

"Why?" she asked bluntly.

He waved his hand in the direction of the water. "Courage Bay's a beautiful place. I feel like taking some time off."

"I don't understand," she said.

"That's all right," he countered. "Your sister never understood me, either. I'm used to it."

She watched in stunned silence as he knocked on the window of the car, waved to Kevin, then walked away.

ANDREA DROVE straight to her parents' home. On the ride over, she kept up a running commentary, partially to see if she could get Kevin to talk, but also to keep her mind off Grant's plans. She wondered just how long "a while" meant in Grant's vocabulary.

She was the only participant in the conversation. Kevin kept silent, his sole form of communication a nod or occasional smile. When she turned onto her parents' street, Andrea stopped a block from their driveway and put the car in park. She knew what she was about to do wasn't the most admirable thing in the world, but with Grant remaining here, the stakes had just been raised. If she could get Kevin to talk to her and her alone, maybe she could find out who was really telling the truth—her sister or Grant.

She turned to Kevin. "Sweetheart, I'm wondering about something that maybe you can help me with…."

He'd been staring out the window, but as she spoke, he looked at her and raised his eyebrows.

"I want to know why you said what you did the other day about the accident being your fault. Did someone tell you that?"

He looked down at his hands.

"Kevin?"

She reached over the seat, took his chin in her fingers and turned his face to hers. "Talk to me. Tell me why you think that."

Pulling away from her, he shook his head.

"If you don't want anyone else to know, we can keep it a secret," she said gently. Raising her hand she painted an imaginary X on her chest. "Cross my heart."

He didn't say a word and once again Andrea had to accept the obvious. He wasn't going to speak to her, at least not right now. She put the car in gear and drove toward her parents' house.

Parking a few minutes later, she looked across the seat once more. "I love you, Kevin," she said softly. "And so do Grandpa and Grandma. You're going to have a lot of people around you who care about you. You know that, don't you?"

With his face still averted, he nodded once.

She patted his leg then got out of the car and walked to the trunk. Taking his crutches out, she came around and opened his door then kneeled down to help him. He reached for her, but instead of pulling himself from the vehicle, he wrapped his arms around her neck and held on tightly. Her heart aching, she cradled his head and hugged him back.

His breath brushed against her ear when he spoke.

"I love you, too, Aunt Andrea. Bunches and bunches."

HER EMOTIONS IN AN UPROAR, Andrea got Kevin settled in her parents' guest room, then said she had to head out. She knew she should tell them about Kevin talking, but once again, she just couldn't do it.

"What's the hurry?" her father asked. "Why don't you stay and visit for a while?"

"I have to go over to Vicki's," she said with reluctance. "Someone broke in the day of the funeral and I have to take care of the mess."

"A burglary?" His expression filled with alarm. "Good grief! Why didn't you tell us sooner—"

"I don't think they actually took anything, Dad. It was probably kids fooling around. They opened some boxes and dumped some stuff out. That's all.

I didn't say anything because it wasn't that big a deal.''

"Did you tell the police?"

"No, I didn't. Grant came in and looked around then agreed with me that we couldn't do more than clean up. There's no way to tell if anything's missing.''

He shook his head in disgust. "Do you need help?''

She put her hand on his arm and squeezed it. "Thanks, Dad, but I can handle this. You and Mom have your hands full now with Kevin. Let me deal with this. I don't mind.''

And she didn't. Entering through the kitchen of the old house twenty minutes later, Andrea put the diet drinks she'd brought with her into the refrigerator then went directly to the dining room. Physical labor was something she'd never been afraid of and she quickly lost herself in the messy process of repacking her sister's things. It took an hour, but when she had everything back in the boxes, she lined them against the wall where they had been before. Pleased with the progress she had made, she decided to keep going. She stopped in the kitchen to grab a soda. Then she walked down the hallway, pausing at Kevin's door before glancing toward the other end. Vicki's room would be the toughest but Kevin's was the messiest. She decided to take the coward's way out and do the office first.

She started with the books, placing them back in the nearest boxes, then moved on to the scattered files Vicki had kept for some of the businesses whose accounting she'd done. Stuffing the folders into a nearby cardboard file box, Andrea forced the lid down then rocked back on her heels and reached for her soda. Instead of taking a drink, she tipped her head back and put the cold can against her throat.

Her gaze went to the ceiling fan and she felt like a fool for not turning it on sooner. She flipped the switch but nothing happened. She then climbed on a chair for a closer look but when her hand hit the metal housing, the light fixture rocked ominously, then tilted to one side. A second too late she remembered that the fan had never been stable. It crashed to the floor beside the chair, scattering bits and pieces of glass and plastic across the room and even into the hall.

That's when she remembered *why* the fan was unstable.

During her teenage years, she'd constantly removed the unused light fixture that had hung down from it. The frosted globe had been her hiding place and she concealed all her contraband inside. Cigarettes. Condoms. Other things she didn't want to think about.

Stepping off the chair with a curse, she kneeled down to start cleaning up the mess and reached for the nearest fragment. Underneath it was a surprise. Her hand froze, hovering above the tiny notebook now revealed.

Good God, had she left something up there all these years?

Her answer came swiftly as she picked up the spiral-bound pad. The lined paper was fresh and white, the cover smooth and clean. It wasn't a relic from ten years before but it wasn't brand-new, either.

Ruffling the pages, she stared at the scribbled diary. Vicki's handwriting covered at least a dozen, maybe more, sheets, her elegant script too distinctive to be mistaken for anyone else's.

Andrea looked up at the fixture in disbelief. Vicki had obviously known about Andrea's hiding place and had taken advantage of it. But why? And when? It seemed strange that she'd leave her boxes packed but take the time to hide this.

A woman's voice sounded from the front of the house. "Hellooo? Hellooo? Anyone home?"

The unexpected noise startled Andrea into action. She stuffed the notebook into the back pocket of her shorts then hurried down the hallway toward the living room.

"CAYMAN STATE BANK. Good morning."

The woman on the other end of the phone sounded British to Grant but there was just enough lilt in her voice to make him think of warm sand and cool water. He and Vicki had been to the Cayman Islands once. Right now he felt as if the trip had taken place in an alternate universe.

He pulled himself out of the past. "Hewitt Belworth, please."

"May I say who's calling?"

"This is in reference to the trust he manages," he said instead of answering her question. He knew he sounded vague but it was the best he could do.

"Oh, yes, he does." Her voice warmed considerably. "Are you interested in making a contribution?"

He didn't know exactly where he was heading, but it'd been Grant's experience that people were generally more helpful if they thought you were going to give them something.

"As a matter of fact, a contribution is exactly what I had in mind."

"Then hold on for one moment, please. I'll find him for you."

The moment lasted less than ten seconds. The possibility of having more money to manage apparently put Mr. Belworth, whoever he was, into high gear.

A squeaky voice came down the line bringing with it thoughts of bow ties and checked pants. "This is Hewitt Belworth. With whom do I have the pleasure of speaking?"

"My name is unimportant, Mr. Belworth, but my money isn't. I'm interested in making a donation to M.D. Ltd. Can you help me?"

"Absolutely." The voice turned unctuous. "We're more than happy to accept anonymous monies. We believe in the right of the individual to distribute his wealth as he sees fit, not as his government would like."

"I understand," Grant answered. "That's why I selected you."

The distance between them couldn't hide Belworth's oiliness—it oozed from both his words and his attitude. "No one supports the structure of the American family more than the Traditional Trust. It's our only purpose and the reason we exist."

Belworth gave up the name of the organization behind the fund just as Grant had been betting he would, but there was no surprise in his revelations. Grant exhaled sharply, his suspicions finally jelling. The Traditionalist Trust was a powerful multimedia conglomerate that controlled everything from magazines and newspapers to local radio stations. To describe them as conservative would be generous.

Their favorite son was Vicki's longtime lover. Pryor Dulcet.

"You're right," Grant said. "The Trust…is the best at what they do."

"And I'm sure you appreciate what that means."

"Money equals power," Grant answered.

Belworth instantly tried to minimize the truth. He chuckled. "Well, I wouldn't quite put it like that, sir. Let's just say we have access to the people who count. And things are looking better every day."

"Especially in California," Grant said carefully.

The man at the other end of the phone didn't disappoint him.

"You're absolutely right, sir, and I must say, if you know that and had this number, too, then you probably know one of our more influential friends out there."

Belworth continued. "I'll see that our mutual acquaintance becomes aware of your donation, sir. Your modesty is admirable, but he'd want to know."

"I'm sure he would be very interested in that fact, however I think I've changed my mind. I'd like to leave the senator a message instead of a donation. If he's smart, he'll realize it's more valuable than money."

"I—I don't believe I understand."

"Tell Dulcet I said he should reconsider his bid for reelection. I've heard it's hard to run a campaign from a jail cell."

CHAPTER NINE

HER WHITE SILK SUIT and highlighted hair seemed over the top and out of place but the woman who stood in the center of the living room clearly wasn't bothered by that fact. To the contrary, when Andrea entered, she was looking around with the kind of supreme confidence and self-assuredness that came from having either money or power. In this case, Andrea thought, probably both.

"I hope you don't mind, but the door was open so I just…" The woman spoke smoothly until her eyes fell on Andrea, then her jaw literally dropped. "Oh, my God," she breathed. "You look just like her."

"I take it you knew my sister?" Andrea walked into the living room and held out her hand. "Andrea Hunt," she said. "And you are?"

The woman extended her hand. "I'm Mary Delaware. And please, forgive my rudeness. I was just so surprised when you came into the room."

"Don't worry about it." She waved off the woman's apology but underneath her polite dismissal, Andrea felt a ripple of confusion. Mary Delaware looked vaguely familiar yet Andrea was sure they'd never met. She put aside her reaction. "What can I do for you?"

"I just heard about Vicki, and I wanted to extend my sympathies. I was out of town last week and when I came back and heard the news, I thought the least I could do was drive down and tell you how sorry I am. Vicki had given me this address so I stopped here first."

Andrea pointed toward the dining room. "Why don't you come in and have a seat? May I get you something to drink? I have some sodas—"

"Nothing to drink, thank you." Sitting down at the table, Delaware shook her head. "I don't really have the time to stay too long. And I've clearly interrupted you."

Taking the nearest chair, Andrea glanced at her grimy shorts and T-shirt. "I was repacking a few of Vicki's things," she explained. "Tell me how you knew my sister."

"We worked together on a charity event," Delaware replied. "A political fund-raiser. I was so impressed with her energy and enthusiasm. We got to be rather close, actually. I was shocked when I heard about the accident."

Andrea couldn't imagine her sister and this woman being friends, much less "close." On the other hand, Vicki had attracted strays of all sorts, rich and poor, animal and human.

Delaware tilted her blond head back toward the living room. "Is that where…it happened?"

Caught off guard by her curiosity, Andrea answered automatically. "Yes, it is."

"Oh, my…" The woman fluttered her hands, then shook her head. "And how is Kevin doing?"

"He's fine. In fact, he's already out of the hospital."

"Oh, that's wonderful." Her expression turned sad. "I guess he'll have to go live with his daddy now?"

The woman's questions were beginning to bother Andrea, friend of Vicki's or not. "He'll be staying with my parents for the time being."

"What about Grant?"

"What about him?" Andrea asked coolly.

"Well, I just wondered…since he's the boy's father and everything…"

Andrea let the woman's question go unanswered. Most people would stutter a bit to fill the resulting silence but Mary Delaware sat perfectly still and waited. She wasn't as scatterbrained as she'd first appeared, Andrea decided. In fact, there was a sharpness to her that could have cut glass.

Andrea stood up. She knew she was being rude, but she didn't care. "I appreciate you stopping by," she said. "But as you mentioned, I am working and there's a lot yet to be done. I'm sure you understand...."

"Of course." The other woman rose in a fluid movement. "I'm sorry I intruded but I had to let someone know how upset I was to hear of her death."

"I understand," Andrea said, walking the woman to the door. "Your condolences are appreciated."

With a thoughtful gaze, Andrea watched Mary Delaware's vehicle pull away from the curb. Her cell phone rang just as the SUV reached the end of the street.

Joe Ripani's deep voice answered her hello.

"I know you were going to take another day off, but we've got a 914A down at the Point," he said without preamble. "How fast can you get there?"

THE MORE GRANT THOUGHT about everything he'd learned, including his telephone conversation with Hewitt Belworth, the more sure he became Vic's death was no accident. He spent the remainder of the day deciding how to proceed, knowing only one thing for certain; he had to be careful, very careful.

Because Pryor Dulcet was a snake. He'd been a state senator for too many years to count and he was ruthless and immoral. No one seemed to notice, though. For years he'd done whatever he'd wanted, consolidating his power into a stronger and stronger base. Like many of his compatriots in the political arena, however, he wasn't very smart. Vicki hadn't cared about his brains, though. She'd been impressed by his power and his money.

They'd been on-again off-again lovers for years, including those she'd been married to Grant.

All evening long, Grant worked the telephone, pushing his contacts in L.A. until he ran out of numbers. Pausing to stretch, he was surprised to see the time—it was almost ten. He gathered his papers and put them away, then walked out to the Impala to go find something to eat. The relentless heat was still present, waves of it rising up from the pavement as he crossed the parking lot. He would have expected the temperature to abate with the sun's disappearance but the air felt even more oppressive in the dark.

He started the Impala, but didn't put it in gear. He really wasn't hungry, he realized, at least not for dinner. Banging his head against the steering wheel, he told himself he was crazy. Then he drove directly to Andrea's house.

Lights still shone in her windows and Grant cussed. Why had he come here? What was he doing? He stared at her front door for several moments, then cursing again, he left the sanctuary of the car and headed up her sidewalk.

Andrea opened the door before he could knock.

Obviously fresh from a shower, she wore a white

terry-cloth robe and a towel wrapped around her hair. Her face was free of makeup and even more interestingly, free of the concern she usually wore around Grant. She clearly hadn't expected him to be on her porch.

But she'd expected someone. She'd opened the door the minute his footsteps had sounded outside.

"I'm sorry," he said, backing up. "I should have called—"

"It's okay," she said, looking past his shoulder. "I thought you were…"

"Someone else," he supplied. "I understand. I'll call you in the morning. I don't want to interrupt."

She put her hands on her hips and shook her head. "Yeah, I have a hot thing going with this guy right here." She nodded toward the street. "You might get hurt if you get between me and him."

Grant turned around to see a teenager walking up the sidewalk. With a pizza box in his hands.

Andrea paid the boy, then held her screen door open. "C'mon in," she said. "You might as well help me eat it, otherwise I'll put the whole damn thing away."

Grant followed her into the tiny bungalow and then into an even tinier kitchen, the smell of hot cheese and pepperoni momentarily distracting him. Suddenly, he was starving. Andrea put the box down on the table, got out plates and forks and told him to sit. She then opened her refrigerator and came back to the table with two cold beers.

They ate in silence, Andrea's appetite matching Grant's. Finishing his beer, he pushed the last piece of pizza toward her and she took it. He liked seeing a woman eat. Every woman he'd been with had always been too worried about her figure to do more than peck at her food, even Holly. Andrea didn't seem to share their concerns. In fact, now that he thought about it, she didn't seem to have much in common with any of the women he'd ever known, including the sister she resembled so closely.

He tapped the edge of his beer can on the table without thinking and she looked up at him, her blue eyes meeting his.

"How can you be so different?" The question slipped out before he could stop it. "How can you look so much like her but be so completely different?"

Andrea didn't reply right away. Instead she blotted her mouth with a napkin, then stared out the window. A hot breeze whispered in and lifted the curtains.

"I can't answer that," she finally said. "We were always very dissimilar, though. I wanted to be the one in charge and she wanted to follow. I guess we just came out that way. As we grew older—and apart—the contrast naturally became more pronounced, I suppose.''

"But you both returned to Courage Bay?"

"Everyone comes home to lick their wounds."

He leaned back in his chair and crossed his arms.

"You disagree?" she asked.

"It's not something I'd do."

"Why not?"

"I'm…not like the rest of my family."

"I thought your dad and brother were cops, too."

"They are," he confirmed. "But they aren't the kind of cop I am. They're cops like…your friend Shields is a fireman. Regular guys."

With her elbows on the table, she propped her chin in her hand and stared at him. "What makes you not regular? And don't say it's because you worked Vice. That's no reason."

He shrugged. "Then I guess I can't answer that question any better than you could answer mine. I'm just different from them, that's all."

She seemed to consider his reply, then she asked unexpectedly, "Do you know a woman named Mary Delaware?"

Grant frowned. "The name isn't familiar. Why?"

"She came by the house this afternoon. She said she was a friend of Vicki's and had just heard about her death. She didn't seem like the kind of woman who would be close to my sister, but she said she was. I remembered your offer at the house after the funeral, and I thought she might be someone you knew.''

''What'd she look like?''

''Money,'' Andrea said promptly. ''Expensive clothes, salon hair, nice makeup. She said she and Vicki had worked together on a political fund-raiser back in L.A.''

Grant held himself still. ''What kind of fund-raiser?''

''She didn't explain.''

''How old was she? Height? Weight? Hair color?''

''Five-five, about a hundred and thirty pounds, blond but not natural.''

He unclenched his jaw—that description matched none of Dulcet's people. ''Sounds like she could be any of Vicki's friends.''

Andrea accepted his reply without comment then dropped her head and rubbed her eyes, her shoulders suddenly slumping. All at once he felt like a jerk. He'd been so busy ogling her he hadn't seen her obvious exhaustion. It wasn't simple weariness that weighed her down, either. Something had happened.

''You had a bad day, didn't you?'' he said softly. ''You should have said something—I would have left.''

Expecting a denial—because that's what Vicki

would have done—Grant was surprised when Andrea bluntly answered. "It was a shitty day. A real shitty day."

"Tell me about it."

She looked skeptical.

"I want to hear," he said.

She shrugged in an okay-but-you-asked-for-it way, then replied.

"Not long ago I volunteered for some special training for suicides. Now, when the problem comes up, I catch the call. Today we had a jumper down at the Point."

"What's the Point?"

"It's a outcropping that hangs over the bay at the southern tip. The drop is bad but the landing is even worse." Her voice went flat. "He didn't make it."

"I'm sorry."

"I am, too," she said. "I was holding his hand when he made his decision. I almost went with him."

Andrea sat for a bit, then she stood and picked up their plates to carry them to the sink. Looking at her slim back, Grant felt his admiration of her rise another notch. She'd been through hell the past few days but she had a job to do and she was still able to do it.

Was she really that strong or was it an act?

Grant took a step toward her just as she turned

unexpectedly. All at once they were nose to nose in the minuscule kitchen.

Her skin was absolutely perfect, he thought in the half second that followed. Smooth and soft. He raised his free hand and touched her cheek.

As if there were others in the room whom she didn't want to hear, she whispered, her breath soft against his face. "What are you doing?"

"Looking for trouble." He could see her pulse beating at the base of her throat. His finger dropped to that point and then he could feel it as well. Beneath his touch, the rhythm seemed to stutter but he wasn't sure. The irregular beat could have been his own, not hers.

"I don't think this is a good place for you to look for that," she said.

"Why not?"

"I don't trust you. I don't want you to take Kevin away. And you weren't good to my sister."

"You should trust me. I love my son. And you aren't your sister."

"I don't know about the first two, but you're definitely correct about that last fact." Her expression shifted minutely. "I'm much *better* than Vicki was at picking out the wrong kind of man." Her eyes swept his face with an intensity that rocked him. "You don't want to go that direction, Grant. Believe me, it'd be a disaster and I've had enough of those."

He turned his finger over and slowly dragged his knuckle over her throat. ''I have a lot of experience with disasters.''

''Then you don't need any more.''

She was right, of course. Grant was crazy to be doing what he was doing and thinking what he was thinking. He considered his options, then he leaned closer and pressed his lips to hers.

ANDREA RETURNED Grant's kiss with a desire that took her by complete surprise. She was unprepared—for his move and for her reaction. When she realized what she was doing, she pulled back, but the feel of his mouth stayed on her lips and she knew later on, when she was alone, it would come back to haunt her.

He continued to hold her. ''I shouldn't have done that,'' he said in a husky voice.

''You're right,'' she answered. ''You probably shouldn't have.''

Neither one of them moved.

''Well, at least we agree on that.'' Without releasing her, he moved his thumb up and down her arm. ''I'm not going to say I'm sorry it happened, though.''

''You don't have to,'' she answered. ''Everyone makes a mistake now and then.''

''I wouldn't call it a mis—''

She stepped back and crossed her arms. "I think it's time for you to leave."

His eyes fastened on hers and she thought he was going to argue. She wondered if she would capitulate, then she realized she wasn't going to need to make the decision. Without saying a word, Grant backed up to the door then opened it and left.

Andrea slumped against the kitchen counter and waited for her heart to slow. When she accepted the reality that that wasn't going to happen anytime soon, she walked into the living room on shaky legs and sat down on the sofa.

She touched her fingers to her lips and stared through the screen door. By the curb, a pair of headlights split the darkness then the twin beams swung around, the car making a U-turn in the middle of the deserted street. Tires squealed as it straightened and then took off.

Knowing she was committing her usual self-immolation, Andrea fought the heat rising inside her. Grant represented what could probably be her worst nightmare, relationship-wise. He was her ex-brother-in-law. The man who had treated her sister like dirt. He wanted to take her only nephew to Los Angeles instead of leaving him in Courage Bay where he could be well cared for, and to top things off, he obviously had a laundry list of "issues," as her therapist would have put it. What did she think she was doing, kissing him like that?

After berating herself for ten more minutes, she wrote off the kiss to stress—both hers and his—then returned to the bathroom where she'd been sorting the laundry when she'd heard Grant arrive. All that was left were the things she'd worn that day. She started to drop her shorts into the hamper, then stopped, feeling something small and hard in the pocket.

She reached inside, then cursed softly. Between Mary Delaware and the suicide rollout, Andrea had completely forgotten about her sister's notebook.

She opened it and read the date at the top of the first page. Vic had started the diary before Kevin was born. Flipping through the pages aimlessly, Andrea felt a wash of guilt as she thought about the kiss she'd just shared with Grant. Before she could chastise herself too much, though, her attention was riveted by a single sentence.

Her back against the tiled wall of the bathroom, she slid to the floor without thinking, clutching the diary as she read.

I never meant to leave Grant, but then again, I never meant to marry him, either.

GRANT HAD PROMISED Kevin a trip to McDonald's and that's where they were going. Pulling into the Hunts' driveway the following afternoon, he wondered if Andrea had told her mother what had happened between the two of them last night. He doubted she had. Vicki would have called Karen the moment he'd driven away, but he had the distinct impression Andrea kept her cards closer to her chest.

Once inside the Hunts' sunny kitchen, Grant felt his concerns ease. Karen and Jack greeted him with warmth and began to brag on Kevin, telling Grant how great he'd been. They clearly enjoyed their grandson as much as he enjoyed their attention.

Grant loaded the little boy into his car and they headed for the Golden Arches. An hour later, Kevin was tired and sated, his Happy Meal gone. Greeting them at the door when they returned home, Jack took one look at his grandson and said, "You need a nap, young man. Let's go!"

The older man picked up the little boy as Karen turned to Grant. "Did you have a good time? Kevin certainly looks as if he did!"

Grant smiled. "The crutches kept him from keeping up with the other kids, but it didn't seem to bother him. He made up for the lack in the eating department."

"After he gets stronger, he'll get a walking cast."

Grant nodded, then said, "Listen, Karen, I really appreciate what you and Jack are doing for me. Keeping Kevin like this…"

"I wouldn't have it any other way," she said. "In fact, I won't lie about it, Grant. We'd like cus-

Play the

Lucky Hearts Game

and get...

2 FREE BOOKS

and a FREE MYSTERY GIFT...

YOURS to KEEP!

yes!

I have scratched off the silver card. Please send me my *2 FREE BOOKS* and *FREE mystery GIFT*. I understand that I am under no obligation to purchase any books as explained on the back of this card.

Scratch Here!

then look below to see what your cards get you... 2 Free Books & a Free Mystery Gift!

336 HDL DZ5X

135 HDL DZ6E

FIRST NAME

LAST NAME

ADDRESS

APT.#

CITY

STATE/PROV.

ZIP/POSTAL CODE

(H-SR-05/04)

Twenty-one gets you
2 FREE BOOKS
and a **FREE MYSTERY GIFT!**

Twenty gets you
2 FREE BOOKS!

Nineteen gets you
1 FREE BOOK!

TRY AGAIN!

Offer limited to one per household and not valid to current Harlequin Superromance® subscribers. All orders subject to approval.

◀ DETACH AND MAIL CARD TODAY! ◀

NO POSTAGE
NECESSARY
IF MAILED
IN THE
UNITED STATES

BUSINESS REPLY MAIL
FIRST-CLASS MAIL   PERMIT NO. 717-003   BUFFALO, NY

POSTAGE WILL BE PAID BY ADDRESSEE

HARLEQUIN READER SERVICE
3010 WALDEN AVE
PO BOX 1867
BUFFALO NY 14240-9952

tody of Kevin ourselves. I'm sure Andrea has told you that—''

"She has," he answered. "But he's my son, Karen, and I don't want to give him up."

"I understand. I want you to think about what that means, though…what it really entails. Are you sure you could handle being a single parent? Here in Courage Bay, there would be three of us for Kevin. If you take him back to L.A. he'd only have you."

"My parents live in L.A."

"I understand that, too." Her eyes filled as she looked up at him. "But we need him, Grant. We need him so much…."

He wasn't a man who was comfortable with outward displays, but Grant took Karen into his arms and hugged her tightly. "We don't have to decide right now," he said. "We've made our arrangements for the moment. Let's leave it at that for the time being, okay?"

She sniffed against his chest, then he felt her drop her arms from his waist. She stepped back and nodded toward the deck. "Have you got time for some coffee? It's cooled off just a tad. We could sit outside…."

Grant had made another list of people to call when he'd come back from Andrea's last night, but he couldn't refuse Karen's sad blue eyes.

"Sure, I've got time," he said easily. "But let's skip the coffee and just sit outside."

"That sounds fine." She led him to the rattan patio furniture. A smattering of papers and note-books covered the top of the low table before the sofa.

"Are you making a scrapbook?" he asked as they sat down.

"I was organizing all the thank-you notes I need to write. Everyone in town sent flowers or plants...."

He pointed to a silk-covered spiral-bound book as he sat. "Is that the guest register?"

"Yes, it is." She picked up the book and held it out to him. "Would you like to see it?"

He flipped to the section where everyone who had visited had signed, quickly surprised to see how many pages had been filled.

He looked up at her. "Have you read all these?"

"I have."

"You don't recall seeing the name Mary Dela-ware, do you?"

"No, but that's hardly one I would have remem-bered, especially not knowing anyone by that name." She paused. "Why do you ask?"

He explained Andrea's mysterious visitor.

"Well, it was nice of her to drive all the way down just to give us her sympathies." She smiled and pointed to another signature. "That was Vicki's fifth-grade teacher. Vicki had such a crush on him...."

Karen's explanations continued but Grant's interest waned. The mystery woman was probably some flake Vicki had bonded with somewhere and she meant absolutely nothing.

He was looking for ghosts because he didn't want to face the facts. He was pretty sure he knew who killed Vicki and he could even guess why. But proving that might cost Grant his own life.

Even worse, it might cost him Kevin.

CHAPTER TEN

AT A QUARTER TO SIX the next morning, Andrea parked her Jeep in the lot opposite the Jefferson Avenue fire house then crossed Fifth Street. She wasn't sure she was ready to go back to work, but after talking to Joe Ripani at the Point, she'd decided she had to. The moment she walked inside the station, she knew she'd made a good decision. It all felt right—the gleaming bays and trucks, the smell of breakfast cooking, even the sounds of someone grunting while they worked out on one of the Cybex machines.

Accepting the other firefighters' condolences was easier than she'd anticipated, too. The ones who had grown up in Courage Bay knew Vicki and had a story about her sister or moment to share. Rhonda simply hugged her. No words were necessary between the two of them. By the time Andrea had made her way to the captain's office, she knew she'd be okay.

With the usual bouts of adrenaline pumping moments interspersed with numbing boredom, the first twelve hours passed. Luckily, it was a fairly busy shift. One chest pain, three wrecks and a premature baby managed to take up most of the time. Still, in between runs, Andrea caught herself thinking of Vicki's diary. She'd put the notebook in her locker, hiding it under a pile of socks as if it were actually worth something.

She alternated between believing every word then discounting it all. The only explanation she could come up with was that Vicki had written the damn thing as some kind of weird practical joke. It *couldn't* be anything else. Because if what Andrea had read was the truth, that meant everything she knew about her sister was a lie.

And everything she knew about Grant was also a lie.

Late that night, when the station grew calm and everything went quiet, Andrea slipped from the bunk room and opened her locker. Removing the tiny book, she tiptoed into one of the stalls in the bathroom, the only place she knew where her privacy would be assured. Rhonda was a great friend but she could ferret out the deepest secret. Andrea didn't plan on sharing Vicki's diary with anyone.

Her fingers shook as she turned the pages again.

Well, I did it. I'm Mrs. Grant Corbin and baby 'Corbin' is on the way. G doesn't have a clue he's not the father.

Seven months later: *The baby's here and I love*

him so much. Once P sees Kevin, he'll come to his senses, I'm sure.

Kevin was almost eighteen months old when the next entry appeared: *Incredible news! P has apologized and we're together again. He promises he'll leave his wife as soon as everything is wrapped up.*

Then this: *I left G this morning but he doesn't know it yet. He won't until he gets home and sees that we're gone. I decided that was the best way to do it. K and I will be with P tonight!*

The last entry was tragic: *It's over. P lied to me again. He didn't really want to be with me the way I wanted—all he's looking for is sex. I thought we could be a* real *family, but P's not interested in that. It's obvious he doesn't want to be a father, and I think he's glad K doesn't talk. He's refused to take us back and I'm sure G's going to do the same. I guess we'll go back to CB and stay there until I can figure out how to make one of them change his mind. What else can I do?*

Andrea leaned her head against the metal stall divider. She felt physically ill.

Her sister had not only lied to Andrea, she'd lied to Grant as well, tricking him into marriage.

Kevin wasn't Grant's son.

ANDREA'S SHIFT WAS ALMOST OVER when a call came over one of the loudspeakers. "Hunt, line 3. Hunt, line 3."

She climbed out of the ambulance where she'd been taking inventory and went to the nearest phone.

"Hunt here."

"Good morning."

Andrea's day was ending but Grant's was clearly just beginning. From the way he sounded, she guessed he'd fallen out of bed and grabbed the phone to call her. His low, throaty voice conjured up an image that was so vivid, she felt as if she'd actually seen it a thousand times before. Pj's riding low on his hips, a bare chest, a shadowed jaw, rumpled hair...

"I have to go back to L.A. for a few days," he said, breaking through her thoughts. "Something's come up. At work," he added. "I wanted to let you know."

A complex cloud of emotions swirled over her. She *had* to tell Grant what she'd read in Vicki's diary. Even though it might devastate him she had a responsibility to see that he knew.

Didn't she?

"Can you tell Kevin why I had to leave? It's too early to phone your parents or I'd call him myself." He hesitated for the smallest of moments. "I...I promised him I'd take him for ice cream later today. Do you think you could fill in for me?"

"I'd love to," she answered, her mind still on

the diary. "My hips might not approve, but when have I ever listened to them?"

Grant's voice seemed to drop—or was it her imagination?

"I don't think your hips have anything to complain about." He paused. "Actually, I don't think any of your body parts do. They all look pretty good to me."

Andrea gripped the phone a little tighter.

As if he could sense her heightened awareness, he cleared his throat awkwardly. "Well…then…I guess that's it. I'm not sure when I'll be back. This might take a while."

"That's fine. Just give me a call when you get here," she found herself saying.

"I will," he said. Then the line went dead. Shaking her head, Andrea hung up, too.

What in the hell was happening between her and Grant?

What in the hell *had* happened between him and her sister?

GRANT WAS ON THE HIGHWAY heading south an hour later. But his mind stayed in Courage Bay.

Every time he spoke with Andrea, the differences between her and Vicki became more pronounced. Vicki would have peppered him with a thousand questions in return for the favor he'd asked. Andrea had simply said "yes." She seemed to have none of the insecurities that had plagued Vicki and he couldn't help but wonder why. Could the same parents raise two daughters who turned out completely different?

He answered himself. Of course, they could. Look at him and his siblings. If he hadn't known better, Grant might have thought he'd been adopted, he was so dissimilar from his brother and sister.

He put the Impala on cruise control and tried to do the same to his mind but as he got closer to L.A. he couldn't ignore the smog and the traffic. Almost in defiance, he let himself imagine a white clapboard house with a picket fence in front. Placing Andrea's image in one of the windows, he was reminded of those television ads about living in a place called ''Perfect.''

Without any warning an eighteen-wheeler came into his lane. Slamming on his brakes, Grant recalled the commercial's punch line: ''But 'Perfect' doesn't exist....'' He then extended his middle finger out his window and cursed as the truck accelerated, muttering out loud, ''No shit...''

Continuing down the freeway, he told himself he'd be crazy in a matter of days if he tried to live in Courage Bay. He was part of L.A. and not the nice part, either. Once they knew who he was, they'd throw him out of Perfect.

For almost a week, he concentrated on finding the information he needed and digging deeper into

Vicki's old life. Every detail he came up with reinforced his suspicions and by Thursday, his course was set.

He headed for the ritzy side of town that morning. Dulcet's office was easy to spot, the building towering over everything nearby, the cars in the underground garage equally impressive.

The shade of the garage should have offered relief from the early-morning sun but the stifling heat it had already trapped was almost worse. Straightening his tie and throwing his jacket over his shoulder, Grant walked directly into the ground-floor offices of the adjacent building. The air that hit him when he opened the door was so unexpectedly frigid, it momentarily froze his brain.

The receptionist had said "Sir?" for the third time before he realized she was talking to him.

For once, his momentary distraction served a good purpose. The secretary/wannabe-actress looked at him with even more disdain than he had hoped for.

"I'm here to see the senator," he said, wiping his brow. "Came all the way from Bakersfield to give him a piece of my mind."

"Do you have an appointment, sir?"

"Well…no, I don't, now that you mention it. Do I need one?"

"If you'd like to see him, yes, sir."

"Then make me one, please."

"You'll have to talk to his assistant to do that. And she isn't here today. She and the senator won't be in the office until the middle of next week. The gubernatorial race is about to get started. They're making a series of town hall visits with the senator's constituency."

Real frustration seeped into Grant's voice. In that length of time, a lot could happen. "Two weeks! Well, dang burn it…" He looked out over the marble foyer and fresh flowers that decorated it then faced the girl again. "When did he leave? And who's running the show while he's gone? And why in the hell does it take so long to visit your constituents?"

"They've already been out three weeks, sir, but I assure you, the senator is still 'running the show.'" She sniffed. "His district is one of the largest in California and that's why he's so busy." Sensing a way to get rid of him, she removed a brightly colored flyer from a nearby stack and handed it to him. "If you want to see him sooner, why don't you visit one of the meetings? This is his schedule. Maybe there will be one near… Bakersfield." She said the town's name as if the word tasted bad.

Grant took the list and scanned it quickly, not believing his luck. All the information he'd come to get was right before him in a neat, word-processed package.

Skipping over the dates, he counted backward to the day of Vicki's death. His finger landed on the name of a town just north of Courage Bay.

He blew his breath out softly, the woman behind the desk forgotten.

Pryor Dulcet had been half an hour's drive from Courage Bay the day Vicki had died. Half an hour. If he'd wanted to, he could have easily slipped out without anyone even missing him, killed her, then returned. It would have been stupid beyond belief for him to actually do it himself, but Dulcet wasn't known for his brains. He had good looks, lots of money and a simple agenda—the preservation and promotion of what he called the one American family.

It would have been easy for him. Then again, most murders were.

Even when the victim was a mistress you shouldn't have had to begin with.

ANDREA CALLED her parents' house around noon. She'd seen Kevin every day she'd been off since Grant had been out of town, explaining the first day that his father had had important work to tend to in L.A. Their afternoon stop for ice cream had become a ritual. "I'll be there at one," she told Kevin now. "Is that okay with you?"

She waited for some reaction, but he said nothing. "Kevin?" she asked a second time.

Karen Hunt answered her daughter. "I don't know what the question was, but he seems all right with whatever you told him."

"That's good."

Andrea had wanted to tell her mother all she'd learned by reading Vicki's journal, but each time they'd talked after Andrea had found it, she'd hesitated. Revealing what she knew would only deepen the wound Vicki's death had already left and Karen wouldn't have been able to explain Vicki's actions anyway. No one but Vicki could do that and she was gone.

Andrea and her mother chatted a bit longer then Andrea hung up, the rest of her morning filled with errands that had gone undone for way too long. After lunch, she found Kevin and her father outside on the front lawn. Andrea watched from the curb, remembering when her dad had gardened with her.

Holding a small trowel, Kevin looked up as she slammed the car door, a huge grin and a smear of dirt decorating his face.

Andrea grinned back. "You look like someone who could use an ice-cream break, what do you say?"

He nodded vigorously then wobbled up, pointing his crutches in the direction of her SUV. "No way," she laughed, grabbing his shirt as he lurched past. "Go clean up, then we'll take off."

With a roll of his eyes, Kevin reversed direction,

and Andrea turned back to her father. "Want to go with us? You look like you could stand to cool off, too."

He shook his head. "No thanks, baby. Your mom has a pitcher of iced tea ready for me. You and Kevin go ahead. I don't need the calories."

His comment made her think of Grant. And thinking of Grant made her think of Vicki. Her expression changed, or so she guessed, her father picking up on her sudden tenseness.

"What's wrong?" he asked. "I can go with you if it's that important—"

"No, no… I was just thinking about something, that's all." Andrea waited a beat, then said, "Dad…did Vicki ever talk to you and Mom about why she returned to Courage Bay?"

Her father rocked back on his heels. "Her only reason was Kevin," he replied, crumbling a clod of dirt through his fingers. "She wanted a good place for him to go to school and have a decent life. She told your mother and me nothing meant more to her than his well-being and L.A. wasn't the place for that."

Andrea nodded thoughtfully, arranging her expression into a semblance of what her father would expect. Clearly Vicki had told their parents nothing of her problems.

Kevin came out the front door and hobbled toward them, precluding any more discussion. Andrea led him to her car and tried to put everything else aside. For the next half hour, the only important issue was what kind of ice cream to choose.

She wished the rest of her life were just as simple.

As IT TURNED OUT, nothing proved to be simple that afternoon, including the ice-cream decision. Despite the fact they'd been there every day for almost a week, Kevin still took ten minutes to pick which flavor he wanted, then he changed his mind twice after that. Feeling the impatience of the people in line behind them, Andrea tried to hurry him along. They ended up getting four scoops, all different.

Things went downhill after that.

Increasingly cranky and out-of-sorts, Kevin didn't like the people who sat down in the booth behind them, he didn't like any of the four flavors, and as time passed, it seemed he didn't much like Andrea, either. It was amazing, she thought as they left the ice-cream parlor an hour later, what the boy could communicate without saying a single word. She buckled him into the car and shook her head. He'd been perfectly all right with her father, but somewhere between the house and downtown Courage Bay, a five-minute drive, he'd chosen to be unhappy.

Deciding she needed to know why, Andrea took him to the beach. The heat seemed to have lessened but even if she were imagining that momentary relief, the bay breezes would still feel good.

Pulling into the spot nearest the water, she cut the Jeep's engine and turned to Kevin. "I bet you haven't even gotten to the beach since you moved, have you? Last time you and your mom visited I think it was Christmas. You probably didn't get to come down then, either."

He pursed his lips and stared out at the water.

"What do you say we walk to that picnic area over there?" Andrea nodded toward a nearby canvas pavilion that shaded a wooden table and benches. "Your mom and I used to sit right there when we were just about your age and have fried chicken lunches. Then we'd go play in the water." Without giving him a chance to agree or disagree, she climbed out of the SUV then went to his side and opened his door. He clearly wasn't thrilled with the idea, but he didn't give her a hard time. They crossed the sidewalk in silence then proceeded down the boardwalk.

When they got to the table, Andrea took a seat on one of the benches but Kevin kept going. A few feet from her, he dropped his crutches then plopped down on the edge of the slatted deck. Andrea watched quietly as he began drawing an intricate pattern in the sand.

He finished his design, then wiped his hand across it. A second drawing began to take shape—

the stick figures of a woman and child, standing hand in hand. Behind them a larger, blocky silhouette loomed. Andrea held her breath. Was he drawing the armoire right before it fell?

She moved to his side, sitting down on the edge of the decking near him. Without a word, she began to doodle in the sand, too.

"I sure miss your mom." Looking over at him, she asked, "I bet you miss her, too, huh?"

He shrugged his shoulders and added a tree to his picture. Then he nodded.

"Did she ever tell you about the time I broke the crystal bell?"

His eyes darkened with interest and he tilted his head.

"Our mother—your grandmother—had a beautiful crystal bell that Grandpa had brought her back from a trip he took to Japan. That's a country a long way from here," Andrea explained. "Grandpa had carried it in a little box on his lap all the way home so it would be safe. It was very fragile."

Andrea leaned closer. "I loved the bell. I thought it was the most beautiful thing I'd ever seen. I wanted to ring it but your grandmother explained it wasn't really that kind of bell. One afternoon she took it out of the cabinet so she could dust. I didn't know the bell was sitting on the table beside her and I ran in the room with the dog to tell her something. He hit the edge of the table with his tail…"

She waited for him to prompt her, but he didn't say a word. "You want to know what happened next?" she asked.

He nodded.

"The bell fell off and broke! Into a thousand pieces. I was so upset I cried and cried. Grandpa had been so careful with the bell and your grandmother had been, too, then I lumbered in with the dog and caused a terrible accident."

She dropped her gaze to the sand where she'd drawn her own picture—the outline of a bell—and the memory hit her. Until that time, Andrea had always thought anything could be fixed. She'd learned that day that wasn't the case.

A seagull cried out overhead and she gave herself a mental shake. Before she could open her eyes and speak, she felt Kevin's fingers slip into her hand.

"It wasn't an accident," he whispered.

Andrea stilled. She wanted to look at him, but she kept her eyes closed, afraid that if she opened them, he'd say nothing more.

She squeezed his fingers. "Yes, it was," she said softly. "I didn't think about it when I let the dog come inside. It wasn't my fault." Despite herself, she turned her head and opened her eyes. "Things just happen sometimes. No one plans them and we don't understand why they take place. That's why they're called accidents. I didn't think about the dog. I didn't see the bell. It just happened."

She waited for him to answer her, to make the connection and talk some more, perhaps about his mother.

Instead he released her fingers and moved away.

Disappointment swamped her but she kept it to herself. Connecting with Kevin was like bobbing for apples—as soon as she thought she had him, he'd drift away again.

They stayed another thirty minutes, playing in the sand and watching the waves. Whatever had made him unhappy at first seemed to disappear, his earlier mood replaced by a quieter, more thoughtful one.

Or maybe he was simply tired.

In the short stretch between the beach and the house, he conked out like a puppy, his arms and legs loose and relaxed, his mouth slightly open. Pulling into her parents' driveway, Andrea glanced toward the sleeping boy. Kids were more perceptive than most people gave them credit for, and the smarter they were, the more pronounced that ability was. He might not talk, but Kevin was sharp by anyone's standards. What had he thought about his mother's antics? What had he thought about the mysterious ''P'' in his mother's diary? Did he know Grant wasn't his father?

She went to Kevin's side of the vehicle and undid his seat belt, slipping her arms around him. As she reached the front door, her mother opened it wide and held a finger to her lips. Once upstairs, Andrea went into Kevin's bedroom where she laid him in his bed, sand and all. Then he opened his eyes. After seeing they were alone, he pulled her closer to him, so close she could feel his lips move when he spoke.

"My father did it."

She leaned back slightly so she could see Kevin's eyes. "I don't understand, sweetie. What are you saying? What did your father do?"

Instead of answering, he closed his eyes and turned his head away. Andrea had no other choice but to leave.

CHAPTER ELEVEN

GRANT DROVE BACK to Courage Bay late on Saturday. The dying sun was low on the horizon but hot rays still managed to stab his eyes.

Putting Dulcet close to Courage Bay the night of Vicki's death had done more than confirm that the distinguished senator had opportunity. The news had made Grant understand, in a way he hadn't before now, the level of Vicki's self-destruction. He'd told her too many times to count that she was running with a crowd that was way too fast. But that's all he'd done.

If he'd really wanted to be effective, he should have taken Kevin away from her, by force if necessary, and by not doing that, he'd let the boy down. Vicki hadn't had the sense of a goose. How could he have expected her to care for Kevin? The child needed stability in his life and someone who loved him, someone who wouldn't let him down.

Now, more than ever, Grant wanted to be that person. But so did Andrea.

An hour later, he was parked outside her house.

A small covered porch stretched across the front, and she stood barefoot on it, poking at something on a grill and frowning. At the sound of the Impala's engine, she jerked her head up and her eyes met Grant's. Any hope he'd had of time and distance diminishing his attraction evaporated. The desire that hit him was stronger than it'd been before he'd left.

He climbed from the car and walked to where she stood. Together, in silence, they contemplated the grill. A charred woodlike piece of meat, he wasn't sure what kind, glowed above the flames.

"Looks tasty," he said after a minute. "Got enough for two?"

She jabbed a long-handled fork in the direction of the item and shook her head in disgust. "I just don't get it. Fixing a meal doesn't seem complicated but I always screw it up."

"That's why there are restaurants," he said. "Put on some shoes and we'll go find one."

She was shaking her head before he finished speaking. "I'm not dressed and it'd take—"

"I know a seafood place down by the docks. It's a dump. Believe me, they won't care."

He picked up a nearby hose and doused the grill. She looked at him for a long moment, then she went inside, the screen door banging shut behind her. In five minutes, she reappeared. She'd put on flip-flops…and lipstick. He'd never seen a woman look better.

An hour later, he watched her peel the last of the barbecued shrimp they'd ordered and hold it out to him.

"If you want this one, it's yours. If not…"

"No, thanks," he said. "My appetite isn't what it usually is."

"I noticed." She ate the shrimp then pulled a paper towel from the roll that sat on the table. Wiping her fingers, she nodded toward his plate. Half a dozen shells littered it, maybe less.

"I think I outpaced you two to one." Narrowing her eyes, she stared at him closer. "You look a little green around the gills. Do you feel okay?"

"I'm fine," he lied. He'd finished off the Cuervo last night, thinking of Vicki and what must have happened. "But if you're done, let's walk." He tilted his head toward the pier. "I could use some fresh air."

She glanced at the iced tea he'd ordered then at her empty beer bottle, a sudden understanding darkening her eyes. Her reaction told him she was no stranger to a hangover but she stood without comment and after he'd paid the bill, followed him out the door.

"You didn't have to do that," she said. "We could have split it."

He shook his head. "I owe you. You took Kevin

out for me and explained everything to him. Consider this a thank-you.''

They headed down the wooden jetty, their footsteps muffled by the sound of the waves pounding the piers beneath them. When they reached the end, she sent him a sideways glance. ''Did you take care of your business in L.A.?''

He turned to look at her. She was leaning against the pier's railing, the wind blowing her hair, the shore lights behind them outlining her profile. He knew he should tell her what he'd learned about Vicki's death, but Grant knew Andrea would want to take it straight to the CBPD. Vicki deserved more than the routine investigation they'd done, and in a way, he felt *he* owed it to her to see that she got better. Once he had Dulcet cornered, he'd bring in the locals and they could take care of the cleanup job. He didn't want their help before then.

''I handled it,'' he said.

''That's good.''

Silence filled the space between them and for just a second, Grant had the weird impression Andrea was hiding something from him as well. He immediately dismissed the idea, telling himself he wasn't thinking straight.

Put in his position, no man between twelve and ninety would have been able to. Andrea stood too close and smelled too nice for a man to think coherently.

''Was Kevin okay while I was gone?'' he asked, mentally switching topics.

''For the most part. He was cranky yesterday but that was understandable. He was feeling sad.''

Grant knew he was supposed to ask *why* his son felt sad, but he knew why. Rather than ask, he estimated the risks of rejection should he attempt to kiss Andrea again.

Before he could finish calculating, she leaned closer to him and flicked her fingers near his ear. ''You have something in your hair. We have these moths out here sometimes—''

He captured her hand in his, stilling her movement and her words. ''Forget about the damn bugs.'' His gaze lingered on her lips, then it came back to her eyes. ''Kiss me instead.''

ANDREA WAS TELLING HERSELF to back away when Grant's lips covered her own but her whole body suddenly went haywire. Even if her brain had been able to send the signal to run, her legs would have refused the order. A mutiny seemed to be occurring.

His mouth pressed firmly on hers, Grant spread his hands on her back, the warmth of his palms passing through her T-shirt. He moved one hand up and the other one down, his thumbs dragging over the bumps of her spine. Each time he touched a different spot, his mouth seemed to do something different as well, his tongue slipping inside and probing gently.

He wasn't kissing her the way he'd kissed her before.

Alarms sounded and her brain went to DefCon 4.

He was her ex-brother-in-law… He'd treated her sister like dirt… He wanted to take Kevin away…

And her personal all-time favorite: *Grant was the wrong kind of man for her.*

Really, really wrong.

But even as the warnings rattled inside her head Andrea felt herself slipping away, the resolve she'd wanted to hold on to fading fast. This was an enormous mistake. She was jumping off the same bridge she'd leapt from before….

Yet all at once, she didn't give a damn.

She returned his kiss with a passion that even took her by surprise.

They made it to the Impala, but just barely.

STUMBLING AGAINST the car door, his arms wrapped tightly around Andrea, Grant thought about the times he and Vicki had been together. Theirs had not been a marriage of love, but they'd had sex, each of them looking for some kind of release. His own needs had been easy to understand because he'd been faithful to Vicki. Most men would have said he was nuts, but married was married…at least to Grant. When Vicki had been willing, he'd been eager. What she'd gotten in return from the encounters, he wasn't quite sure. He hadn't wanted to ask.

This was much, much different.

Andrea continued to hold on to Grant as they climbed in the Impala's back seat. After that, all he was aware of were her hands, her mouth, her body… He almost felt as if he were underwater, somehow swimming through the night with nothing more than her touch to guide him. He closed his eyes and let the feeling carry him until he realized what he was doing, then he turned things around. Kissing her deeply, he pushed up her shirt and then pushed aside her bra. Taking her freed breasts in his hands, he continued to kiss her, his mouth dropping lower until he pulled in one nipple and sucked, then turned to the other and did the same.

When he slid his hand inside her waistband, she moaned deeply. Feeling the same need reverberate inside him, Grant began to tug off her shorts.

ANDREA CAME TO slowly, an awareness of her surroundings the first sensation to register. The second one was a feeling of disaster.

Halfway on the seat, halfway on top of Grant, she froze and looked at him. "What are we doing?" she asked.

His right hand was threaded through her hair and as she spoke, he tightened his fingers. "I thought we were about to make love." He paused. "But something tells me I'm wrong...."

She edged away from him, the back seat too small for the storm of emotions taking place inside her. "I...I don't think that's such a good idea."

"It seems like a pretty good one to me."

She shook her head. "It'll just complicate things. And they're already crazy enough."

He shifted, his eyes meeting hers. "What kind of things?"

"Well, for starters, what about the redhead? Vicki told me you were having an affair with someone at work—"

"That was over before I met Vicki."

"I need the details. Is she...still in the picture?"

"No." Her blouse hung open. He reached out and drew a line down the center of her chest, his fingers brushing the lace of her bra and the tops of her breasts. "Vicki knew that, too."

"What's her name?"

His expression was patient. "Holly Hitchens. She *is* a redhead and a detective but we're just friends."

His explanation rang with truth, and suddenly self-conscious, Andrea straightened her clothing.

"Okay," she said slowly. "But what about the other obstacles?"

"Like what?"

"You were married to my sister."

"That's irrelevant."

"Not to me."

"Why?"

"It just seems strange."

"You hardly knew me before the accident, Andrea. We were basically strangers."

"That's true, but you knew her and now you know me. I don't want you comparing us."

He rubbed her bottom lip with his thumb, then pulled her hand to his mouth and kissed each knuckle. Besides being erotic, his touch was incredibly tender. Andrea steeled herself against it.

"I'm past that," he said softly. "You're too different from her for that to even be an issue. Apples and oranges. Black and white. Day and night."

She relaxed—even though she didn't want to.

He drew her close again, his breath warm against her skin as he kissed her once more. "Vicki may have looked like you, but you're nothing like her, Andrea. I didn't understand that at first, but I do now, and you should, too."

As he spoke, Andrea decided this sounded like the truth, as well. She touched his face, then said, "Are you different, too?"

He frowned in obvious confusion.

"The way Vicki talked about you before she

died…'' Andrea paused, uncertain of how to proceed. ''You don't seem like the same man she described. You're much…more…'' She couldn't find the right word.

He waited in silence.

''Let's just say I hated you for what you did to her and to Kevin.''

''But she was lying.''

''I understand that now.'' She hesitated, took a deep breath, then added words that stopped his heart. ''I'm beginning to think that wasn't all she lied about, either.''

HE'D BEEN WRAPPING a strand of Andrea's hair around one finger but as she spoke, Grant froze. ''The last time I tried to tell you that, you told me I was wrong. That Vicki never lied to you. Never.''

A look of regret passed over Andrea's features. Was it because she'd said something she hadn't meant to or because she had found out the truth?

''I wasn't thinking straight before,'' she hedged. ''No one tells the truth all the time. Life doesn't work that way.'' She moved across the seat again, putting herself out of reach.

Remembering his suspicions back at the pier, Grant wondered what she was hiding. He debated the option of simply asking her, then he thought about Kevin and held his tongue.

She tilted her head then repeated herself, as if trying to distract him. "*Are* you different?"

"No one stays the same forever so I guess I'd have to say 'yes.'"

"Is that good? Or bad?"

"I don't know," he answered. "I think you'll have to be the judge of that."

Their passion broken, they rode back to Andrea's home in silence, the windows down, the night air rushing past until they turned onto her street. Grant slowed then parked in front of her house. Just as before, Andrea sat quietly and stared through the window.

Grant waited for the awkwardness that always came to him during a moment like this but it didn't materialize. Instead he found himself wishing he could follow her inside. And finish what they'd started.

He leaned over and tugged at her chin until she faced him. The minute he saw her expression he knew what he wanted wasn't going to happen. She'd closed herself off from him.

"It would have been okay, Andrea." He dropped his fingers to her throat, the urge to kiss her coming over him so powerfully, he wasn't sure he could fight it and win. "Don't be upset…"

Her eyes gleamed in the darkness. "That's not what's bothering me," she said. "I'm scared because I wish we *hadn't* stopped."

GRANT HAD BEEN GONE an hour. Andrea had checked her e-mail, cleaned up and showered. Unable to postpone her thoughts any longer, she now lay in bed, stared at the ceiling and told herself she'd done the right thing.

Not only would making love with Grant have been crazy, it would have been stupid…the kind of stupid that Vicki had specialized in, not Andrea. Impulsively stupid. Nutty stupid. Irresponsibly stupid.

Despite her admonishments, Andrea continued to replay the encounter. She remembered how Grant's hands had looked on her skin and how his lips had covered hers. She thought about the way his biceps had curved and how the muscles in his back were hard and straight. Even the scent of his hair stayed with her—it'd smelled like a new bar of soap.

The memories of the physical encounter would fade but Grant's tenderness would stay with her a very long time. If she were a bigger fool than she'd already proven herself to be, she might even believe he cared for her. She knew better than to think that, but for just a moment—a single, solitary second—she let herself pretend. Smart, handsome, responsible…he had all the right equipment. In another life, in another place, Grant might be a man she'd actually consider.

Andrea closed her eyes with determination. When she'd been a kid she'd distracted herself by concentrating on sounds. She'd been able to mentally take herself somewhere else by simply closing her eyes and listening to the bird calls outside her window. She tried this now, but the birds didn't cooperate. She only heard silence and the questions that plagued her.

Why hadn't she told him about the diary? She'd had plenty of opportunity and he needed to know. Was she trying to protect him for some stupid reason?

Rolling over restlessly, she tucked her hands beneath her cheek and stared at the wall beside her bed. Patterns of light and dark, made by the street light and night breezes, skated across the stucco, changing forms continually. Flashes of Grant mixed with images of Kevin and her mind became even more tangled.

Finally she got up and went out her back door. Hidden from the street by a ring of dense bamboo, the tiny porch just off the rear of the house offered privacy and fresh air at the same time. Thinking the latter might help, she sat down on the aluminum patio furniture that had been there when she'd moved in, tucking her feet beneath her nightgown.

Her mind turned to Kevin and his words from the last time she'd seen him.

Her storytelling skills were obviously in need of improvement. She'd been convinced Kevin would catch the connection between her childhood accident and his mother's death, but he hadn't gotten it. Was there another way she could get him to see he'd had nothing to do with Vicki's death? Andrea tried to come up with a different solution but all she could do was think about the rest of their conversation, bits and pieces of it floating into then out of her consciousness.

Kevin *had* to understand he wasn't responsible for his mother's death. That kind of thinking could do lasting damage to his psyche. Maybe Grant could help her think of a way to get that across to him.

Kevin would listen to whatever his father had to say. Except for the one incident at the hospital, they seemed very close. The memory of that episode triggered another thought, and then another. Out of the blue, Andrea suddenly recalled Kevin's whispered words from their day at the beach.

It wasn't an accident.

She sat straight up, her bare feet dropping to the concrete as her brain spun in a convoluted circle. Covering her open mouth with her hands, she shook her head and tried to convince herself she was wrong. "No." She took a deep breath. "No. No. No." Saying the words failed to make the idea leave.

It wasn't an accident.

How on earth could she have been so blind, so stupid?

It wasn't an accident.

Had she been so attracted to Grant, she'd lost her mind?

It wasn't an accident.

The metallic taste of fear flooded her mouth and Andrea began to shake.

It wasn't an accident. My father did it.

CHAPTER TWELVE

AFTER THAT, sleep was out of the question. Andrea stayed awake the rest of the night, or at least for what was left of it, finally dressing around five. She went to the phone a thousand times to call the police department, but each time she picked up the receiver, she ended up putting it back. What kind of evidence did she have that Vicki had been killed?

None.

And what kind of evidence did she have that Grant had done it?

None.

All she had were the words of a troubled child who spoke to no one but her. She'd be laughed out of the police station.

Vicki's death had already been ruled accidental. Andrea doubted the examiner would look kindly on a lowly EMS attendant questioning his report. It might even cost her her job. If she wanted to find out more, she had to do it herself and do it discreetly.

But work came first. She'd already told Joe she

wanted to make up some of her lost days and she'd
picked today to start. She went to work early, yet
her brain stayed on one thought. Had Grant killed
her sister?

Logic kicked in and more questions were raised.
Why would Grant even want Vicki dead? Was the
fact of her affair enough to push him to murder?
There were logistics to consider as well. Would
Grant have had enough time to kill Vicki then drive
back to L.A.? Andrea had called as soon as she'd
been able but when had he received the message
that Vicki had died?

As the day progressed, she developed a plan of
action.

She was on the phone, dialing LAPD when the
shift's first call came in. A multiple vehicle accident
on Link Street. She and Rhonda tore out of their
bay in record time, Rhonda behind the wheel. They
sped to the scene and arrived three minutes later,
bailing from the ambulance to run toward the
pileup. Three cars had been involved and things
didn't look good.

By the time they'd tended to everyone and transported the injured, it was almost five. Rhonda spoke
as she backed the ambulance into the bay. ''God,
I'm starving…it isn't your turn to cook tonight, is
it?''

Andrea didn't respond except to shake her head.
When the truck was parked, Rhonda put a hand on

Andrea's arm. "You okay? You're awfully quiet today."

"I guess I'm tired."

"Big date last night?" Rhonda teased.

Andrea denied the question so vehemently that Rhonda became suspicious and for the remainder of the evening, which included a broken leg and a possible overdose, peppered Andrea with questions. It was past ten o'clock before she managed to convince Rhonda she was telling the truth and escape her watchful eye.

Heading for the phone in the Haz Mat office, Andrea had little hope of catching the person she wanted to talk to this late, but she had to try.

"LAPD—Hollenbeck Station."

She faltered for a second, then gathered herself. "I need to speak to a detective by the name of Holly Hitchens, please."

"She's gone. Wanna leave a message?"

Andrea's shoulders slumped. "No. I'll call back tomorrow."

Her only answer was a click. Hanging up the phone, she stared at a report titled ANTHRAX PROPHYLAXIS, TREATMENT AND REPORTING GUIDELINES.

What in the hell was she supposed to do now?

WHEN GRANT STOPPED at the Hunts' the following evening to see Kevin, Karen opened the door and smiled with delight. "Grant!" she said. "Perfect timing! We're just about to eat."

"Then don't let me interrupt. I just wanted to say hi to Kevin and leave these." He held out a cellophane-wrapped bouquet of light-pink roses. "They reminded me of you when I saw them at the store."

"Oh, Grant..." Her eyes filled as she took the flowers. "You shouldn't have done that...but I'm so glad you did. I insist you join us for dinner and don't even think about saying no. We're celebrating the removal of Kevin's big cast and he's dying to show you how he can walk in the shorter one."

The aroma drifting from the backyard promised something more appealing than what Grant had planned on having for dinner but it also reminded him of Andrea and her grill. He'd tracked down the hotel where Dulcet had stayed the night of the murder, but other than that, thoughts of blond hair and blue eyes and smooth, soft skin had occupied him. When he'd stopped to get the flowers for Karen, he'd bought condoms, too. If he got the chance to use them, he'd be surprised, but he never would have thought he and Andrea would have ended up in the back seat of his car, either.

Karen took his arm and pulled him inside without waiting for an answer. When Jack and Kevin walked into the hall a moment later, Grant couldn't believe the changes in the boy. Kevin looked great.

Tanned and rested, he sported a much smaller walking cast and there was a sparkle about him that said he was a kid again and not a little person with worries he shouldn't have. Grant's chest loosened with relief. He hadn't realized how anxious he'd been about Kevin. As the burden fell away, though, he realized something else.

The Hunts had turned Kevin's world right side up. Not Grant.

All this raced through his mind while Grant accepted Karen's offer then shook Jack Hunt's hand. Oblivious to his father's concerns, Kevin headed toward the kitchen. When Grant didn't follow, the boy paused, looked back over his shoulder and motioned impatiently. The excitement on his face was unmistakable.

Jack laughed and tilted his head. "He's got something special to show you. Been saving it since Monday."

Grant started to follow his son, but he took two steps and stopped. Coming out of the den to his right, Andrea did the same.

"Grant—"

"Andrea—"

They said each other's names simultaneously, but Grant recovered first. "I didn't realize you were here...."

A flash of tension crossed her face and her voice, as she answered him, was strained. So strained, it told him she regretted what they had almost done and the conflict over Kevin was about to get worse.

Jack unintentionally interrupted the awkward moment. "Are you two going to stand there and gab all night or are you going to come look at this boy's surprise?"

Andrea started forward, Grant falling into step beside her as they went down the hall and toward the back of the house. He could almost see her nervousness. He wanted to pull her aside and talk but that wasn't going to happen. At least not while they were here.

They reached the laundry room. In addition to the washer and dryer, it held a small freezer. As Grant and Andrea entered, Kevin opened the door to the unit and pointed grandly inside, a look of pride plastered on his face.

Andrea put her hand on her chest. "Oh, my God! What a giant fish!" She looked at her father. "Did you stop at the Seafood Shoppe and buy it? How did you get one so big?"

Kevin's eyes rounded and for one heart-stopping second, Grant thought he was actually going to say something. He kept his silence, though, and gestured wildly, pointing toward himself and the fish. When he mimed the act of throwing out a fishing line, Andrea shook her head. "No way! Are you telling me you caught that fish?"

Leaning closer to the freezer, Grant spoke up.

"Of course he caught it! Kevin would make a great fisherman. He can do anything, can't you, buddy?" He bent down to Kevin's level, putting one knee on the tile floor. "What is that? It looks like a red-fish…"

Moving closer and closer to Grant, Kevin ended up sitting on his father's knee, his silent conversation continuing. As Grant wrapped his arms around the boy's shoulders and hugged him tight, he heard Karen call out from the kitchen.

"Enough on the fish already! Can I get some help in here?"

Jack rolled his eyes and disappeared, leaving Grant, Kevin and Andrea. Grant turned to Andrea and started to speak, but she backed out of the room. "I'd better go help, too," she said.

A second later, she was gone.

If Jack and Karen sensed the strain between Grant and their daughter, they kept it to themselves. Over dinner, they chattered comfortably, asking Andrea about her work and Grant about his office. By the time Karen brought out ice cream, though, Grant had had enough. Examining Andrea's every move for hidden meaning had left his nerves raw and edgy. He had to escape.

Promising Kevin he'd return the following day, Grant said his goodbyes and thank-yous, then asked Andrea to walk him to his car. They both knew she couldn't refuse without looking rude. She shot him a look across the kitchen island, then said, "Sure."

When the front door closed behind them, she walked quickly down the sidewalk, clearly anxious to have him gone. Catching up with her, Grant tugged her to a stop. They stood in the dark, her perfume floating around them. He had difficulty concentrating on what he had to say, because all he wanted to do was kiss her.

As a consequence, he didn't mince words. "Despite what you said Saturday, I get the feeling you wish you'd done something else than spend time with me."

She licked her lips. It was a nervous gesture he hadn't seen her use before. "I'd say we did a bit more than 'spend time' together."

"I thought women preferred euphemisms when it came to that particular activity."

"Not this woman," she said. "I say what I mean."

"All right," he conceded. "Then how about this? Tell me what the hell's bothering you and don't say 'nothing' because you'd be lying."

"It's…complicated," she finally said.

He pulled her closer, ignoring her token resistance. Her mouth inches from his, Grant stared into Andrea's eyes, then he kissed her. Slowly. Carefully. Completely.

"What's so complicated about that?" he asked when he finished.

"You know what I mean," she said levelly. "Don't play games with me."

"I don't do that. Games are for kids. We're grown-ups."

"That's true," she replied. "And we ought to know better. What we almost did the other night was impulsive and dangerous."

"Then I was right. You wish you hadn't jumped in the back seat with me. You *are* having second thoughts."

"I didn't have any *first* ones, and that's the problem."

"Thinking is overrated. It isn't always the right thing to do."

"And why is that?"

"Sometimes the answer you come up with isn't the one you expect. Then you're stuck with even more questions than you started with."

Within the circle of his arms, she stiffened. "What the hell does that mean?"

"Your sister didn't think about anything before she did it. You go the opposite direction. You think too much." He paused, his gaze tracing her lips before he lifted it. "That might get you into hot water one of these days."

She twisted out of his embrace and took a step

backward, another strange expression coming over her features.

"It's too late for *might*." She shook her head and took a second step. "I think I'm already there."

Standing on the sidewalk, Grant stared in surprise as she fled into the house. If he hadn't known better, he would have thought she was scared of him.

THE STRAIN OF GETTING through the evening must have shown on her face. Andrea's mother insisted she go home and get some sleep.

"You look exhausted, darling." Making a sweeping motion with her hands, Karen said, "Go on! Your father and I can clean up. Kevin will help."

Andrea briefly wondered how her mother would react if she knew what was really on Andrea's mind. No doubt she'd tell Andrea she was crazy... and she could have been right.

Andrea bent down to look at Kevin. "Do you think you could do my part of the dishes?"

He nodded, a serious determination darkening his eyes.

"I guess anyone who could catch a fish like the one in the freezer could definitely handle some kitchen work, huh?"

He nodded again, then smiled, his elation over his prize still too fresh for anything—including chores—to dampen his spirits.

She kissed her parents goodbye then drove straight to her place. It was almost nine. Since she'd left the station that morning, she'd repeatedly tried to get Holly Hitchens on the phone but had had no luck.

Sitting beside Grant at dinner and carrying on a conversation had been difficult to say the least. If her mother had warned her he was coming, Andrea would have stayed home. Instead, the questions that had bothered her all day had continued to plague her through dinner. Could he have been involved with Vicki's murder? Was he capable of murder? Had he known his wife had been having an affair?

Watching Grant interact with Kevin, Andrea had almost decided she *was* insane. No one could possibly treat a child with the tenderness he did and be a killer, too. The two of them had a very special relationship: Kevin *couldn't* have seen Grant push over that armoire. If he had, he wouldn't have let the man near him.

Then she had walked outside with him, and he'd said what he had.

She shivered as she remembered his hooded eyes and the unforgiving grip he'd had on her elbow. In his car the other night, she had concentrated on the gentleness of his touch, the smoothness of his hands. She recalled more memories now. Like the way his fingers had tightened in her hair. The way his teeth had nipped her neck. The way he'd pinned her to the seat. Had his actions been the result of unguarded passion or something else? Something darker? Something more dangerous?

You think too much. It might get you in hot water one of these days.

His words couldn't have been interpreted as anything but a threat.

Parking her car, Andrea went inside and headed directly for the telephone in the kitchen. She dialed the LAPD number from memory and asked for Holly Hitchens one last time. If the detective still wasn't in, Andrea was going to have to find another way to get her answers. She couldn't waste any more time.

Just as before, the desk transferred her call but this time, to Andrea's shock, a woman answered. "Hitchens here."

The voice matched Andrea's image of a redhead named Holly. Sultry, sexy, curvy...

Andrea gripped the phone so tightly her palms began to sweat. She didn't have a clue as to what to do next. Blurting out "where was Grant Corbin when his wife died?" didn't seem to be the best course of action but she wasn't too sure what was.

"This is Hitchens," the woman repeated. "Who is this?"

Andrea spoke quickly, knowing if she didn't, she might hang up instead. "Hello, Detective Hitchens.

I'm afraid you don't know me but my name is Andrea Hunt. I'm the sister of—''

''Grant's ex,'' she said with an edge. ''He mentioned you when we had dinner the other night. In fact, there were only two topics on his mind. One was his son and the other was you.''

Andrea thought the cop's voice held a note of jealousy, but that was such a ridiculous thought, she dismissed it and forged ahead. ''Detective, I know this may sound a little confusing but I need to ask you something,'' she said. ''Something about the day my sister died.''

''I don't know how I can help, but go ahead.''

''I was wondering if you saw Grant that day.''

A tick of silence came over the line, then the detective said one word. ''Why?''

Thank God, she'd rehearsed this, at least. ''I wanted to know who told him about Vicki. I called right after it happened and left a message at the station, but I never had a chance to thank whoever delivered it. I was too rattled to tell him myself.''

Another pause followed, then the woman spoke again. ''I'm the one who told him. The captain thought I should handle it because Grant and I were…friends.''

''I understand,'' Andrea said evenly. ''Then thank you very much. I appreciate you doing that for my family and for Kevin. By the way, what time was it when you told him? He must have really driven fast—''

There was no pause this time. Holly Hitchens interrupted her. ''What is it you want to know, Ms. Hunt? If you would come out and ask, you would make life a lot simpler for both of us.'' The detective's voice went from curt to sarcastic. ''If you're establishing his alibi, don't worry. It's rock solid. I saw him the night before as well as early the next morning. He wouldn't have had time to drive down there and get back.''

Andrea stuttered a reply. Later she couldn't remember what it was, but it must have made some kind of sense because Holly Hitchens returned her goodbye and hung up. Andrea went to shower, more bewildered than ever. Holly and Grant might no longer be lovers but clearly the detective still cared for him. Had she lied or had she told Andrea what had really happened?

If Grant was not Vicki's killer, then who was? The only answer Andrea could come up with was the obvious one, but it made no sense. Why would Kevin's biological father, whoever he was, want to kill Vicki?

Twenty minutes later Andrea lay in bed, her mind tumbling over the possibilities of her next step, dismissing half of them before she even let them completely form. Go to local police? Tell her parents? Continue on her own? Finally a single realization emerged from the chaos.

If she wanted to uncover the truth, then Andrea had to tell Grant the truth.

About his marriage…and his son.

CHAPTER THIRTEEN

GRANT STARED out the window of Pat's Pancake House, the chipped plate beside his elbow dotted with the remnants of cold scrambled eggs and toast. There were better places in town to eat, like the Courage Bay Bar and Grill, but he didn't feel comfortable there. The one time he'd gone to the restaurant, too many strangers had come up to his table and offered their condolences. He'd felt awkward and hadn't known what to say.

He turned back to the list he'd started the night before and checked off his points one more time.

Vicki had been having an on-again-off-again affair with Pryor Dulcet for years. If it ever came to light, the publicity would destroy Dulcet's career, Kevin's existence even more so.

A car had been seen at Vicki's house the night of murder. A car that was linked to the Traditionalist Trust, a fund that supported Dulcet. Dulcet had been in one vicinity of Courage Bay that night, too.

Dulcet was a tall and powerful man, an ex-football player. More than capable of pushing over the armoire if angry or upset.

Motive, opportunity, means.

Dulcet had all three, but Grant needed ironclad proof if he wanted to take this any further. Vicki's death had been ruled accidental—he had to have some physical evidence to get that overturned and the case reopened.

Unless he took a different route.

He sat for another hour and thought. Then he stood up, threw a wad of dollars on the table and headed to the pay phone at the back of the diner. Having seen it too many times on his own damn phone bill to ever forget, he dialed the number of the senator's personal line.

Dulcet answered immediately, clearly expecting a call. He'd probably already replaced Vicki, Grant thought coldly.

"This is Pryor. What can you do for me?"

Grant had never heard him speak so playfully. The distinguished senator's public demeanor was much more serious and rational, a better fit for the Family First speeches, Grant decided, than this one, which he kept private for obvious reasons.

"Very little," Grant answered. "But you could do a lot for me. I seriously doubt you will, though. Helping me would entail being honest and you're not so good at that, are you, Senator?"

The voice dropped. "Who is this?"

In the mirror hanging next to the phone Grant caught his reflection. His smile wasn't pleasant. "I'm the one who talked to your buddy at the Traditionalist Trust. I'm the one who knows what you've been up to. I'm the one you have nightmares about."

The man at the other end began to bluster. "Look here, I don't know how the hell you got this number or what you want, but I don't have time for this kind of nonsense—"

"I'm sure that's right," Grant answered. "You're too busy screwing other men's wives."

"What the—"

Grant loosened his grip on the phone and forced himself to step back. He couldn't get too hot or he'd lose his advantage.

"You've done something you shouldn't have, Senator. Something a little more serious than your usual transgressions. I think you know what I mean." Grant paused. The silence from the other end was tense. "I want you to think about what you did, then I want you to think about the fact that I know."

"If it's money you want—"

Bingo, Grant thought. Now he knew where Vicki's big bucks had come from. "This isn't about money," he said harshly. "This is about murder."

He didn't give the other man the opportunity to

reply. "Take a few days and think about it," he said harshly. "I'll be in touch."

With that, Grant hung up.

Dulcet was rash and impulsive. If Grant had rattled him enough, Dulcet might self-destruct.

With a sense of satisfaction, Grant crossed the parking lot, then climbed into the Impala and headed for Vicki's house. On top of everything else, he'd been thinking about the break-in. Whoever had done it had been looking for something important. Feeling lucky after the conversation with Dulcet, Grant thought he might just find what he'd missed before.

His thoughts turned to Andrea as he drove. She had acted strangely during dinner last night and something told him her actions weren't because of what had—or rather hadn't—happened in his car. He'd tried to call her later but her phone had been busy.

The possibility came to him from out of the blue.

What if Andrea knew what Grant had just told the senator…that Vicki's death had been a murder?

If she'd somehow learned the truth, it didn't take a genius to make the next leap. She'd wonder who had killed her sister. Then she'd think of him.

And head straight for the nearest police department. By the time the dust had settled, no judge in Courage Bay would even dream of giving custody of Kevin to Grant, the truth be damned.

He didn't want to believe the thought that followed. Maybe Andrea was setting him up. Maybe
the episode in the Impala had even been part of it.
She *was* Vicki's sister, after all.

He'd been manipulated by Vicki so many times,
it'd been second nature for him to distrust her.
Thinking Andrea was different, he hadn't bothered
to keep up his guard. He could list a dozen times
when Vicki had gone to extremes to get what she
wanted.

Would Andrea do the same?

He remembered that night on the pier. She'd
been hiding something then and he'd known it.
He'd known it but he'd let it pass because he'd
been too busy thinking with something besides his
brain.

Anger—at himself and at her—washed through
him in a hot wave.

His hands gripping the steering wheel, his
thoughts in turmoil, Grant pulled up to Vicki's
house ten minutes later.

Andrea's Jeep was in the driveway.

ANDREA HAD BEEN at the house for a little less than
an hour when she heard someone knocking. Her
head jerked up from the box she'd been repacking
and her heart began to race. She'd come here on
the pretense of cleaning up a bit more but in reality
she was hiding from what she had to do. Sooner or

later she had to talk to Grant but she'd decided this morning she preferred later.

Her reasons were simple. The more she thought about it, the more convinced she became that the stranger who was Kevin's father was also Vicki's murderer. She'd seen flashes of Grant's anger but he wasn't a killer. If she'd been thinking straighter, she would have realized that right away.

Just as she'd feared, when Andrea opened the door, Grant stood on the porch, his jaw locked, his stare unblinking. Intimidating didn't begin to describe his demeanor, and suddenly she realized something she hadn't noticed before. Grant didn't need a weapon. His stance, his attitude, even the suspicious way he looked at her all seemed threatening. Why she hadn't seen this until now she wasn't quite sure.

"Grant..." Her hand went to her throat. "I... wasn't expecting to see you here."

Stepping into the entry, he passed her silently and she closed the door. When she turned, he was right behind her. They were so close she could smell him—shaving cream and soap—and the sensation rippled over her, leaving her without breath. Her legs actually started to tremble. Partially from nervousness.

Partially from desire.

He slowly removed his sunglasses and looked at her. "What are you doing?"

"I was getting these things ready for storage. What are *you* doing?"

"I'm looking for something." His eyes were flat. "Something important. It's called the truth and I think you've been twisting it."

His words jarred her as much as his attitude. "I don't know what you're talking about," she said. "But I don't think I like the implication."

He took her elbow and guided her into the den where two lone chairs filled the empty space. He led her to one of them, then stood above her as she sat. For a fleeting moment, she knew how the people he arrested must feel. It wasn't good.

She tried to stand but he kept his hands on her and walked behind her, kneading the muscles of her shoulders. If she hadn't been so uneasy, the massage might have been pleasant.

"You told me the other night not to play games with you and I told you I didn't do that." His voice was silky. "Do you remember that conversation, Andrea?"

She tried to look at him, but he held her firm. "Of course I do!"

Grant made the circle around her chair, then he knelt in front of her, his hands sliding down her arms then lower, to her thighs. She had on shorts and he slipped the tips of his fingers just inside their hem. She knew he would feel her trembling.

"I'm glad you remember. Because it's time for

the truth. You've been hiding something from me since the day I arrived and I want to know what it is.'' His fingers tightened on her legs. ''Right now. Right here. Tell me your secret, Andrea, or I'll uncover it by myself.''

SHE BLINKED in the hot dusty silence and her blue eyes—the blue he could never forget—seemed to change. Vicki's had always stayed the same; Andrea's became darker when she got upset.

''I don't like being bullied.'' She stared at him steadily. ''If you're trying to scare me, forget about it.''

He could hear the anxiousness behind her words even though they sounded brave. He called himself a bastard, but he didn't stop. ''You have to tell me what you're hiding. Give it up, Andrea.''

She hesitated, then a second later, he felt the tension go out of her legs. Her shoulders slumped. ''You aren't going to like it.''

''Just tell me,'' he said. ''*I'll* decide how I feel.''

He let her pull away. She stood and walked across the room to the uncovered window, her footsteps reverberating with a hollow sound. When she spoke, her voice sounded just as empty.

''I found Vicki's diary,'' she said, her back to Grant.

Grant sucked in a sharp breath. The diary. Dammit it to hell… He should have remembered it! Like a teenager with nothing better to do, Vicki had always been scribbling in the damn thing. Dulcet would have wanted it, of course. He had to have been the one who'd broken in.

A momentary satisfaction washed over him, then the *real* importance of Andrea's revelation registered. His chest tightened until he couldn't breathe.

God almighty... If she'd read the diary, Andrea had to know everything.

Grant stood and came to her side. Harsh sunlight poured through the glass and highlighted her face. Her eyes glimmered in a way he'd never seen before, and his heart fell out of his chest.

"You read it?" The question was unnecessary.

She nodded slowly.

"I did read it, Grant." She put a hand on his arm and spoke in a halting voice. "Maybe I shouldn't have, but I did."

"So you learned all her secrets?"

"Yes." Andrea blinked. "I'm afraid I found out some of yours, too."

He didn't curse or sigh or give her any indication that he understood. He simply stared at her.

"Her diary laid out everything, Grant. Her life...when she was married to you and afterward, as well. I don't know how to even begin telling you what it said."

"Then maybe you shouldn't."

"I have to," she said. "There are things you need to know. Important things."

"Like?"

"Before I get into that, there's something else I have to tell you first." She closed her eyes as if gathering her thoughts, then she opened them and spoke. "I don't think Vicki's death was an accident, Grant. I think someone pushed that armoire over on her and Kevin. Vicki was murdered."

Even though he'd considered the possibility—only minutes before, in fact—that Andrea might have begun to have suspicions about her sister's death, surprise must have crossed his face. He'd been expecting her to tell him about Kevin's father.

Her expression grew pained and she seemed to flinch. "I'm sorry, Grant," she whispered. "I know it's hard to believe but—"

"Tell me why you think this."

"There are several reasons, some of which I read about in the diary, others that…came to my attention later."

"Such as?"

"Well, for one thing, Vicki's body was face-down, her feet next to the armoire. She was looking away from the case. Something about the setup bothered me at the time, but I didn't realize what that meant until the other night. If she'd been trying to attach the earthquake brackets to the armoire as

I originally thought, she would have been standing the other way.''

''Maybe she saw it falling and wanted to push Kevin to safety. That's what the examiner put in the autopsy report.''

''I know what he wrote, but he was wrong. She couldn't have moved that quickly. There's more, though.''

He waited.

''It has to do with Kevin.''

''Go on.''

She swallowed hard. ''He…he's talked to me, Grant. Several times now.''

Grant hadn't expected that. ''He…he's spoken to you? Out loud? Why in the hell didn't you tell me?''

''I don't know why I kept it to myself, but I just did, okay?'' She looked aggravated at his interruption. ''That's not what's important, though.''

''Not import—''

''What matters is what he said.'' She put her hands on Grant's arms. ''Kevin told me Vicki's death wasn't an accident, Grant. I didn't understand at first, but then I put it all together.''

This conversation was turning out a lot different than he'd expected. ''Dammit, Andrea—''

''I thought he was talking about something I'd told him—a story about my childhood—but then he kept going and…and said something else.''

Grant stared at her.

"He said his father pushed over the armoire and I believe—"

Grant froze, her words hitting him with the force of a slap. In the stinging moment that followed, his brain sped out of control, and then his cynicism took over.

She was doing exactly what he'd thought...she was playing him for all she was worth. He gripped her arm fiercely.

"I'm not going to let you get away with this, Andrea," he growled. "I swear I'll—"

She jerked away from him and took a step backward. "'Get away with this?'" She repeated his words in confusion. "I'm telling you the truth, Grant! In Vicki's diary—"

He interrupted her. "Why the hell would Kevin say something like that? I don't understand—" As he spoke, a sick rumble started in the bottom of his gut, and Grant broke off abruptly. With Vicki, anything was possible...but surely she wouldn't have told Kevin that Dulcet was his "real" father? He was way too young to understand that.

Grant's heart pounded as he forced his eyes to Andrea's. "What did Kevin say?" he asked tightly. "What were his *exact* words?"

She clearly wanted to move the conversation in a different direction, but she stopped and answered his question. "His exact words were 'My father did it.'"

Closing the distance between them, Andrea put her hands on his arms. Her fingers dug into his biceps painfully.

"Grant, that's what I'm trying to tell you. When Kevin first said what he did, I assumed he meant you, but the truth of the matter is much different." She drew a breath, held it, then let it out slowly, her painful words coming with it. "Vicki was having an affair with a married man. She didn't refer to him by name in the diary so I don't know who he was. It started before you got married and it…it continued even afterward." Her eyes filled with the kind of fleeting regret he'd wished a thousand times he'd seen in Vicki's gaze, but never had.

"Kevin's not your son," she said softly. "His father was her lover. And whoever he is, I think he killed my sister."

GRANT'S REACTION stunned Andrea.

He stared at her in silence, his face a steel mask, his body a stone pillar. He showed no emotion whatsoever.

"Did you hear me, Grant? I said Kevin's not your son—"

He pulled away from her with a rough jerk. For half a second she thought he might hit her and she winced in advance.

Instead he turned his back to her and cursed.

She reached out to touch him once more, but she dropped her fingers without making contact, too unsure of everything to continue.

"I didn't want to tell you but I…I had to," she said. "If this man is somehow involved in Vicki's death, we need to find out who he is, what he does, where he lives…"

"Is that the only reason you want to find him?"

She frowned in confusion. "Isn't that reason enough? Good God, Grant, I just told you—"

"I know what you told me." He pivoted, his expression so fierce she sucked in her breath. "I heard you the first time. Answer my question, dammit!"

"I—I…yes, of course!" she stuttered. "That's the only reason! What other reason do you need? Isn't that one good enough?"

"It might be for some people, but you *are* Vicki's sister. Somewhere along the way, I let myself forget that fact. What kind of a price am I going to pay for my negligence? Since you're collecting, I assume it's going to be a steep one."

Stunned into silence, Andrea stared incredulously at him. Finally she was able to speak. "I just told you Kevin wasn't your son and Vicki was murdered, and you're attacking my motives? Are you crazy? Why do you give a damn about this other stuff? Don't you care about what I said?"

Grant's voice vibrated with a barely contained fury. "You can think whatever you like, Andrea, but don't underestimate me. The *only* thing I give a damn about is Kevin. Finding his biological father won't help your case one bit. I'll see you in hell before I let you use this information to take him away from me."

The venom in his words slid down her spine and she put her hand to her chest. Her heart beat crazily beneath her fingertips, then understanding hit her. She felt herself blanch.

"Good God, this isn't part of that battle, Grant! I wouldn't—" She broke off, then spoke again. "That's another matter altogether. I didn't *want* to tell you Kevin isn't your son or that my sister cheated on you. I knew it'd hurt you but I thought you should know the truth because I want justice for Vicki. Don't you…don't you care about that? How can you just ignore what I've said?"

He took a step toward her and she had to force herself to stand her ground.

"I'm not ignoring anything. But everything you've told me is old news, Andrea. I've known it all from the very beginning."

CHAPTER FOURTEEN

"You knew?" Andrea felt her eyes go wide. "H-how did you know? Why didn't you tell me? I should have been told this sooner—"

"Don't." He held up his hand. "Don't even try. *You* should have told *me* everything you knew the minute you understood it."

"I had to make sure!" she protested. "I wanted to protect Kevin."

"So do I!" His voice thundered against the bare walls and ricocheted back. "That's what I've been saying, dammit! I only care about Kevin!"

In the throbbing silence that ensued, Andrea stared into Grant's eyes and the comprehension of who he was—who he *really* was—came over her.

He was a good and decent man who had cared so deeply about giving a child a name and a daddy that he'd married a woman who had never loved him. He was willing to fight for that child, as well, with everything he had in his power. Just as he'd told Andrea, all he'd ever wanted was the best for Kevin.

And from the very beginning, she'd misjudged him.

Andrea blinked rapidly, but her tears welled up and fell unchecked to slide hotly down her cheeks. Grant cursed out loud. Then he crossed the room and folded her into his arms.

THEY ENDED UP AT Grant's motel. It was neutral ground and when he suggested they go there, Andrea had agreed. She felt numb and empty as he parked the car then led her inside.

Beneath a single window, the air-conditioning unit blasted away, stirring the dusty draperies that hung above. Grant strode across the room and switched it off, turning to Andrea as silence descended.

His dark eyes were unreadable in the single shaft of light that fell through the slit in the drapes, yet when he came to her side and lifted his hand to her face, his emotions were as clear as if he had spoken of them.

"I should have told you about Kevin," he said softly. "But I was scared—"

She put two fingers over his lips. "Don't," she whispered, repeating his earlier command. "We both did what we thought was right. That's the important thing."

He studied her face for lies, and finding none, he bent to kiss her. When he lifted his lips from hers,

Andrea felt dizzy with confusion. She clutched a handful of his shirt to steady herself. ''Where do we go from here?'' she asked.

He enveloped her in his arms and pulled her head to his chest. She hesitated briefly, stiffening inside his embrace, then she melted against him.

They sank to the bed together and a moment later, her T-shirt and shorts were lying on the floor, her underwear following. She reached for the buttons on his shirt but Grant captured her hands in his then slowly moved them above her head. When he began to kiss her, she understood. He wanted to heighten his own pleasure by first denying it. She found this unbelievably erotic and as his mouth drifted from her lips to her neck, the last of her inhibitions fled.

His hands never left her body and during the ensuing hour, he teased her relentlessly with his touch. Just as she thought she could take no more, he'd bring her to a climax then let her down slowly. A moment later, the torture would begin again. Aching for real release, she rolled him beneath her and straddled his hips, taking control.

His clothes joined hers on the floor and they started all over again. She danced her fingers over his chest, then lower and lower still, the drape of her hair giving her privacy where none was needed. When she finally took him in her mouth, he pulled the silky curtain away and held it back. He wanted to watch and the realization brought her to another climax, without him even touching her.

He didn't last as long as she had. After only a few moments, Grant moaned and lifted her to him, kissed her deeply and entered her at the same time.

She held her breath then let it go, their rhythm building. When the end came, she closed her eyes and cried out loud.

AFTER THEY FINISHED making love a second time, Andrea rolled to the side of the bed and pulled the clock closer. It was a little past one in the afternoon. With a groan, she reversed directions and found herself face-to-face with Grant. His eyes narrowed lazily. ''I'm three years older than you, baby. You gotta give me some more time if you're ready again.''

Despite all her worries, Andrea found herself smiling. ''Okay,'' she said, ''ten minutes, tops. How's that?''

He lifted a hand and brushed her cheek with the back of one knuckle. ''How 'bout five instead?''

Pulling up the sheet, Andrea answered him but in the back of her mind she was thinking about something else. She was wondering what it would be like to have a man like Grant really love her. *Really* love her. The wedding/family/house of their own kind of love. Had Vicki not understood how lucky she'd been? How could she have been so blind to her own good fortune?

Andrea had no idea who he was, but the married man her sister had been involved with couldn't have come close to Grant. Grant was a man with integrity and he loved a little boy who wasn't even his own. She closed her eyes and thought of Kevin and how Grant had been afraid she might use the fact of the boy's parentage to her advantage. If the truth was ever revealed, it'd be devastating to all concerned.

She came out of her reverie to feel Grant's lips on her shoulder. He kissed her softly then got out of bed and walked into the bathroom. Ten minutes later they changed places, Andrea replacing Grant in the shower. When she came out, wrapped in a towel, he was already dressed.

"I ordered coffee," he said as she reached for her clothes. "And some sandwiches."

She nodded and returned to the bathroom, Grant's voice drifting through the open door as she dressed.

"We need to talk," he said.

He sounded serious. She tugged on her underwear and then her shorts and top. Pushing the door with her foot, she combed her hair with her fingers and looked at his reflection. His expression matched his tone and she knew immediately what the topic of conversation was going to be.

"About Vicki?" she asked.

Their eyes met in the mirror. "Yes," he said and stood up. "About Vicki." He stopped short of entering the bathroom and leaned his shoulder against the door frame. "You were right. She was murdered."

Andrea nodded slowly.

"And her boyfriend probably did it." He paused. "I've been checking him out and it's more than possible he was at her house that night. Mrs. Moore saw a car and I managed to link it back to him."

Andrea turned away from the mirror. Grant had been reciting the facts so dryly it took a heartbeat for understanding to sink in. She steadied herself on the nearby towel rack. Her voice was stunned. "You know who he is...."

"Yeah, I know him." His expression was grim. "I've known for years. His identity was not one of Vicki's secrets."

She stared at him.

"His name is Pryor Dulcet," Grant answered quietly. "He's a California state—"

"—senator," Andrea said numbly. "I saw one of his campaign posters in Vicki's office but I just thought she'd liked the poster. I had no idea...."

"She was Dulcet's mistress when I met her. I was working an extra job, a security gig for another senator, and Dulcet came to one of his fund-raisers. Vicki was with him, although few knew they were a couple. When it came time to leave, the crowd had grown and the people in charge needed help getting her and Dulcet out. A week later, she called to thank me. It went from there.''

''And when she got pregnant?''

He returned to the bed, the mattress sagging when he sat down on the edge. Andrea followed him, taking the small armchair under the window.

''She came to me and said Dulcet's wife wouldn't give him a divorce, even though he'd asked her for one repeatedly. Vicki said he was tied to Morgana financially, but he'd told Vicki she was his one true love.''

''Do you believe that?''

''Of course not…and neither did she, deep down. But part of her still thought he'd leave Morgana if she got pregnant because he and Morgana had no children. Vicki was obviously wrong…money keeps those two together.''

''So you knew all along that Kevin wasn't your son.''

''Yes, I knew.''

''But you never let on to Vicki?''

He shook his head. ''No, I didn't.''

''Why not?''

''I didn't *want* her to know. Vicki was ditzy, but she was smart, too. She would have wondered why I stayed.'' He stood and began to pace the stretch of carpet in front of the bed. ''I didn't want to have to explain that I was in love with her and I wanted to help. I thought that maybe…'' His voice died and he checked his stride.

''That maybe she might fall in love with you?''

''Pretty pathetic, huh?''

A flame of heat flared within her. ''Yes, actually, it is,'' she said distinctly. ''It's real pathetic. Because if my sister had had half a brain she might have seen how fortunate she was. Instead, she chose the wrong man.'' Andrea shook her head with disgust. ''God, why do we do these things?''

In the silence, she felt Grant's stare. He seemed stunned by her simple words, but he didn't comment on them or question her. With a determined look, he continued his story and resumed his pacing. ''One way or the other, that's what I thought. And of course, I was wrong. We tried—or at least, I did—but the marriage was doomed from the beginning. Vicki wanted out. I let her go and she went back to Dulcet. But it didn't work. I'm not sure why.''

''I am.'' Andrea picked up the story. ''She explained it in the diary. She called him 'P,' and wrote that he'd said his wife still wouldn't cut him loose and he had to stay. She seemed to finally accept that the relationship wasn't going anywhere. That's when she and Kevin returned to Courage Bay. The diary stopped at that point. Maybe she tried one last time to reconcile with him, but when he came to see her, they fought instead. And she died.''

Andrea waited for the lump in her throat to subside, then she waited for Grant's reply. When it didn't come after a minute, she glanced up. He'd stopped pacing. Frozen in a spot just to the left of the bed, he stood perfectly still. Looking closer, Andrea saw that he was far away, at least in his mind. Another ache came over her for what her sister had done to him.

He came out of his trance slowly, blinking as he did so. ''That's it.''

Andrea frowned. ''That's what?''

He shook his head, blew out a breath, then cursed. ''Vicki must have realized he wasn't going to ditch his wife and marry her. Ever. She got him to the house, then laid it on him.'' He met Andrea's questioning eyes. ''She was blackmailing him. *That's* why he killed her.''

His declaration shocked her but not enough to make her lose her logic. ''You have no proof of that! Where's the money if that was the case?''

He told her about the sixty thousand and she blinked.

''All right,'' she conceded, ''maybe that explains the cash, but it still doesn't make sense. Why now after all those years together? If Vicki had wanted to blackmail him, she would have already done it.''

''She didn't have reason to before.''

"And what was her reason now?"

"There were two very good ones," Grant said. "Until this point, she'd loved him. When she realized he'd been using her, she felt rejected. And angry. She wanted to get even."

Andrea's mouth went dry. "And the second reason?"

"She'd finally come to understand that he was *never* going to marry her because his political situation was about to change. The receptionist at his office practically spelled it out for me and I was too dumb to get it." He paused. "Pryor Dulcet's about to run for governor. A mistress and an illegitimate child aren't the kind of baggage you want to take on a trip like that. He *had* to get rid of her."

THE PLAN CAME TOGETHER almost without thought.

Grant leaned over the desk and took Andrea's hands in his. Her fingers were cold and her eyes nervous.

"Are you sure you want to do this?" he asked. "It's not a game, Andrea. Dulcet's a big guy and he's obviously playing for keeps."

"I can handle him." She spoke with confidence. "You find him and set it up. I can do the rest."

"When he knows you have that diary, he'll be here in a hurry. With a bagful of money, too." Grant looked out the window beside the desk. "I should have realized what was going on when I phoned him this morning.''

''You talked to him *this morning?*''

Grant nodded. ''I called him just before I went to the house. I wanted to rattle him. He started to say something like 'if it's money you want,' but I blew him off. Obviously, he's already worried. When he couldn't find the diary, he must have realized someone else had it.'' As he spoke, Grant's eyes went to the clock beside the bed. ''Damn! Is that clock right?''

Andrea looked over her shoulder and nodded. ''What's wrong?''

''I told Kevin I'd pick him up this afternoon and take him to the beach. I was supposed to be there ten minutes ago.''

''Then we'd better get going.'' Rising to her feet, Andrea grabbed her purse and started for the door. ''He doesn't like it when you're late.''

She was right.

When they arrived at the Hunts', Kevin was on the front porch wearing his swimsuit and a frown. As Grant and Andrea came up the sidewalk, however, Kevin's displeasure seemed to evaporate, and within a few minutes, Grant understood why. Kevin greeted him with his usual enthusiasm but it was Andrea he couldn't stop looking at.

They loaded into the Impala and headed straight for the shore, Kevin bailing out the minute Andrea finished wrapping his cast in a plastic bag. Wearing her shorts and T-shirt, Andrea played in the gentle surf with the boy, yelling and splashing as if she were six herself. Grant sat in the sand a distance apart and watched them, his heart turning inside out.

Andrea was the one who knew Kevin didn't like tardiness. And her father was the one who had taught him how to fish. As for everything else, Karen Hunt did it and did it perfectly. She was, after all, his grandmother. The facts were obvious. Kevin's life was more than complete…without the man who wanted to be his father.

THEY MADE AN EARLY NIGHT of it since Andrea had to go to work the next morning. Grant dropped her off at Vicki's old house so she could pick up her Jeep, then he and Kevin drove away. They said they were going straight back to her parents' place but Andrea had a sneaking suspicion they were going to make one more stop…at the ice-cream parlor.

She jumped into her vehicle and hoped she was right. Spending time with Grant was good for Kevin—he needed the kind of male role model Grant could provide. Suddenly, she found herself worrying what would happen when the situation changed and Grant went back to L.A. Before this point, she'd seen the problem only from her side— now she considered Grant's position. Her parents would be more than happy to share Kevin with him, she was sure, but taking a kid out on Sunday to the cafeteria for lunch produced a very different relationship than did living with him day after day. Feeling disloyal to her parents, Andrea knew too many guys at the station who only "visited" their children instead of helping raise them. It was sad for everyone concerned.

But, God...his lovemaking had left her thoughts swirling. She'd never been with another man who cared so much about what *she* felt, rather than his own pleasure. Grant had been so selfless and loving, she'd lost her bearings, and the dizziness still lingered. Her breath quickened as she remembered his hands on her skin, his mouth on her body. She pulled herself together and tried to focus on the road.

After she got home, Andrea cleaned up then made herself a cup of tea and went outside to the porch to finish her thinking. The sun had dipped beyond the horizon and the air felt heavy and ominous. Distracted by some rumbling thunder, she felt her thoughts wander. When the weather went bad, the team's work tripled. Car wrecks, domestic disturbances, slips and falls...everything got worse, and she felt an uneasiness come over her.

She took a sip of tea. Maybe it wasn't the weather that was disturbing her so much as it was Grant's revelations. Through them, she'd begun to understand Vicki wasn't the person she'd thought she was. Grant had turned out to be a completely different man than she'd first assumed, too. It was disturbing to realize her judgment had been so far off the mark.

The shadows around her grew as deep as her concerns. If she'd misjudged her own sister and someone she'd grown as close to as Grant, then where else had Andrea gone wrong? All along she'd thought the best thing for Kevin was to stay with her parents, but with her mistakes so fresh in her mind, she found herself questioning that now, too. Sighing heavily, she stood up to go inside. She wasn't going to solve the problem tonight.

To her surprise, sleep came easily. The alarm sounded at four-thirty and by five-thirty, she'd eaten her breakfast, showered and dried her hair.

If Grant's plan came together quickly, she might not have time to come back to the house. She needed to be prepared and take everything with her to the station…just in case. With that in mind, she headed for her bedroom. The space was tiny, her bed taking up most of the area without leaving a free spot for even a dresser. Most of her clothing was kept underneath her bed in a low plastic container.

Removing the box, she lifted the lid and felt around in one corner, her fingernails scratching the bottom. When she'd finished reading the diary, she'd hidden it inside a cap then tucked the cap at the back of the box. Feeling foolish hiding it, yet too anxious to leave it in plain view, Andrea had known it'd be safe. Even if someone broke into her home—something that never happened in her neighborhood—she doubted they'd look here for valuables. On the off chance they did, they'd think nothing of a beat-up notebook.

So why wasn't she finding it?

A tremor of uneasiness snaked down her back. Yanking the case closer, she turned it upside down and dumped everything out. Lingerie, shorts and tank tops...it all tumbled to the floor in a heap. Andrea patted down each article, turning the pockets of the shorts inside out and even unfolding her bras and panties.

The notebook wasn't there!

Throwing the container behind her, she got on her belly and lifted the bed skirt to peer underneath the mattress. Nothing but dust greeted her. She crawled to the wall just to make sure, coughing and sneezing as she patted the floor all around her.

She wormed her way from underneath the bed. Beneath her anger was a chill of fear. Someone had been in her house and she hadn't even known it. When had he come? Had it been Dulcet himself or had he sent someone else? Andrea pondered the questions, but in the end, only one thing mattered.

How could she and Grant lure Dulcet into a confession if he'd already stolen their bait?

CHAPTER FIFTEEN

IN THE END, Grant decided the best way to handle the setup was in person.

Early Wednesday morning he drove to L.A. and headed straight for the senator's office. Sitting across the street in a small diner, Grant watched as Dulcet showed up shortly before noon. An hour after he arrived, a convoy of half a dozen or so of his fellow senators parked before the building and went inside. Accompanying them was a woman Grant recognized from the photographs in Dulcet's campaign propaganda. She was his wife, Morgana Dulcet.

As tall and powerful-looking as the men around her, Mrs. Dulcet was dressed in a black pantsuit that probably cost twice Grant's monthly salary, her jewelry heavy and gold, her face as smooth as a ball bearing. Grant found himself wondering how much she knew about the sixty grand he'd found in Vicki's checking account. Morgana's family had funded Dulcet for years but Grant seriously doubted if their largesse would extend to blackmailers.

Grant finished two more cups of coffee then the men and Dulcet's wife left. Another cup and the senator's black SUV pulled out of the underground parking area. Grant followed it to the private gym where Dulcet had a standing weekly game of handball scheduled. What he didn't yet know was that his partner wasn't going to show...because Grant had called *his* assistant and informed her that Senator Dulcet had had to cancel because unfortunately something had come up at the last minute.

The something unfortunate was Grant.

He parked a few rows from the senator's vehicle and watched him go into the facility, his suit coat thrown over his shoulder, his walk jaunty. He was going to be the next governor of California, his attitude said, so he'd better be treated right. He came out ten minutes later wearing a scowl.

Dulcet yanked open the driver's side door of his high-end SUV and started to climb in. At the very last minute, he saw Grant, now sitting in the passenger side. If his hand hadn't been holding on to the steering wheel, the man would have fallen down.

"Wh...what the hell..." he sputtered. "Who are you? What are you doing in my car? Get out of here before I..." As he spoke, his eyes narrowed, then recognition hit.

"That's right," Grant said softly. "I'm who you

think I am. Now get in the damn car and start it up. We're going for a little ride.''

ANDREA GRIPPED THE TELEPHONE in the Haz Mat office and cursed in frustration. She'd been trying to get Grant since six that morning and so far had had no luck. All she got on his cell phone was his voice mail and no one answered in his room.

The station's loudspeakers suddenly blared from overhead and the dispatcher's tinny voice sounded. "904B. 904B. Meet the officer at the dock. 907K. 907K."

Andrea's pulse kicked into high gear. A boat was on fire at the marina. The ladder truck was needed and paramedics as well. She burst out of the office and ran straight for Bay Three and the ambulance. Racing out of one of the bathrooms, Rhonda jumped in on the other side a second later and they took off down Jefferson Avenue, the truck ahead of them, sirens screaming, lights flashing.

Steering the cumbersome vehicle through downtown traffic as if it were a sports car, Rhonda got them to the docks in ten minutes flat.

They didn't have to wonder where the fire was—a plume of smoke led them straight to the second pier. Rhonda slammed to a stop, threw the ambulance in reverse and backed up, gravel spewing from beneath the tires as Andrea called in their arrival. She then grabbed their standard go kit and

Rhonda snatched everything else. Feet pounding on the wooden deck, they raced in tandem toward the still burning boat, Alex's crew of five already hauling their unrolled hoses in the direction of the pier.

As she neared the end of the wooden walkway, angry voices reached Andrea over the chaos. She took in the scene with a sinking sensation. Separated by a single Courage Bay police officer with hands outstretched, a man and woman were screaming furiously at each other, their gestures wild. Each wore signs of having attacked the fire or perhaps each other. Their clothes were torn and dirty and his arms were red to the elbow. One of her legs bore a long bloody scratch.

Violence frequently broke out when EMS teams responded, especially in the larger cities where gangs were involved. In Courage Bay, as in most places, the root of the problem usually sprang from drugs or alcohol, sometimes psychiatric disorders. The trouble here looked like a combination of all three.

Andrea dropped her kit and rushed toward the officer. The teams had a standard protocol for handling these situations but like the joke went, the situations were never standard. She and the officer exchanged looks and nods, Andrea taking the man by his arms as the female cop did the same with the woman. Pulling the combatants in opposite directions, Andrea and the policewoman managed to bring down the yelling to a level that was somewhat understandable.

"What's this all about, sir?" Andrea tilted her head toward the smoldering boat. "Is that your boat?"

"You're damn straight it is," he spit. "But she thinks she should have it." Beer fumes wafted toward Andrea. "She's not gonna get it, though! I'll see it burn in hell before I let her take it!"

Andrea reached out to calm him again but he shook off her hands and grabbed his crotch instead. Raising his voice again, he screamed over Andrea's shoulder. "You already got these!" He shook himself for emphasis. "What else do you want, you bitch?"

"Now, sir, please…" Holding back an unintentional grin, Andrea took his arm and led him farther away. They came to a stop and she said, "Please…you have to calm yourself. Screaming like this isn't going to help matters."

"And what will?" he said bleakly, his voice so hoarse she could hardly understand it. "Tell me what will help! I let her have everything I had and she still wants more! The house, the kids, the cars— I gave it all to her when she asked for her 'freedom.' Now I find out she wants my boat, too. So she and her sweetie there can go out for a little spin?" He shook his head. "I don't think so. Look at him,'' he said bitterly. "He could be her son, for God's sake."

Without meaning to, Andrea swung her head around. Standing near the edge of the crowd that had gathered, she easily spotted the kid in question. He was in his twenties, dark hair falling over one eyebrow, his tanned stomach ripped. A guilty expression on his young features.

Andrea turned back to the man, pity rising. "That may be the case, sir, but this isn't the way to go about solving the problem. We have lawyers and courtrooms for that. They're much better at that than fire trucks and paramedics."

"I'd like to kill her," he muttered darkly. "That's what I'd really like to do. I'd like to wrap my bare hands around her bony throat and—" He stopped and looked at Andrea with puzzled eyes. She started to ask him what was wrong, then a strange expression crossed his face. A second later, he grabbed his chest and collapsed at her feet.

GRANT GAVE DULCET directions and the senator put the big SUV in gear and started driving.

"You're a busy man," Grant started, "so I'm going to make this fast. I have something you want…or maybe I should say, something you need. I'm willing to trade for it."

Dulcet's hands tightened on the steering wheel,

his knuckles going pale. "I don't know what you're talking about."

"Okay, then. Stop here." Grant pointed to a nearby park. "I'll get out and when the shit hits the fan, you can fend for yourself. Right over there," he gestured. "That'd be good."

To his surprise, the senator pulled over but when Grant reached for the car door, Dulcet spoke shakily. "Wait. I—I…" Falling silent, he licked his lips.

Grant gave him a few seconds, then said, "Time's up." He yanked the padded leather handle and stepped outside the car.

Dulcet reached for Grant's arm but his fingers grabbed air. "Stop!" His hand dropped as Grant paused. "Don't be so hasty," he blustered. "Tell me what you've got then I'll decide what I want to do."

"*You'll* decide? This isn't about *you*." Grant's expression hardened. "It's about Vicki."

"Vicki's dead," he said brusquely. "And what went on between the two of us is history."

"Not exactly."

The other man's eyes flickered.

"She had your son, or have you forgotten that small fact?"

"Kevin isn't my child."

"Don't dick around, Dulcet. I know the truth.

And with DNA, the rest of the world can know it, too.''

"You wouldn't do that," Dulcet sneered. "A big bad cop like yourself, tell everyone he's been played? I don't think so."

"Then think again," Grant said stonily. "Because I don't give a damn. I've never stood in front of ten thousand people and told them how mighty my morals are and how theirs should be the same. Nobody gives a rat's ass about me." He paused. "You aren't in the same position as I am, though. I don't think your wife would be too happy to find out you have an illegitimate child. And the Traditionalist Trust folks would drop you so fast, you wouldn't know what hit you."

The senator faced the windshield and stared toward the lake in the center of the park. Grant could almost hear his brain scrambling to find a way out. When his neck began to turn red, Grant spoke.

"I have a simple solution."

"I'm sure you do." Dulcet's words came out from behind clenched teeth. He waited as long as he dared, then he turned to Grant. "Get in," he said harshly.

With perverse pleasure, Grant took his time. When he slammed the door, it sounded like the lid closing on a coffin.

"I have the diary," he said without preamble.

"Give me the same amount of cash you gave Vicki and in return, I'll see that the notebook disappears."

"What makes you think I paid her anything?" Dulcet asked.

"I saw her bank account. Don't act like an idiot."

They stared at each other over the plush leather seats, the hostile silence between them growing thick.

"How do I know you'll stop there?" Dulcet asked finally.

"You don't," Grant answered. "But if you go along and act nice, I'll throw in a little bonus." He leaned closer, as if about to tell a secret. "I won't turn you in for special circumstances. Kevin was there and he almost died, too. That would mean the needle, Dulcet. Are you willing to risk it?"

Dulcet paled. "Look, here, Corbin, it's not like what you think—"

"You're full of shit, Dulcet. I know what you did and I have proof—beyond the diary." Grant let his words sink in, then he spoke harshly. "It's gonna cost you to see it disappear. The only question is how do you want to pay—in dollars or with your career?"

"This is crazy!"

"I agree. I can't remember the last time a senator got put away for murder."

"You bastard…" Behind Dulcet's bravado, his

voice shook slightly. "You're a cop, for God's sake. A cop! You can't do this to me."

Grant smiled nastily. "I already have."

BY THE TIME Rhonda and Andrea returned to the station, it was early afternoon. Andrea tried to call Grant but just as before, no one answered either phone. With a disappointed sigh, she hung up and started for the kitchen. She could hear the others when she was halfway down the hall.

"You should have seen Andie's face! Her expression was priceless…" Rhonda was laughing so hard, Andrea could barely make out the words. "'What else do you want?'" she asked in a deepened voice. "'You already got these…'"

Andrea and Rhonda had stayed at the hospital until it was clear the angry boat owner wasn't having a heart attack. They'd both been concerned. The man had had enough trouble.

Andrea entered the kitchen with a mock frown. "You shouldn't be making fun of Mr. Peterson like that. The poor guy's lying in the hospital right now."

"Yeah, that's right…" Rhonda took a bite of her ham sandwich. "He suffered a wicked attack of indigestion after setting his boat on fire! Who wouldn't?"

Usually the first one to participate in the jokes and backslapping typical of all fire departments,

Andrea grinned but she left it at that, drifting toward the fridge to make herself a salad. All she could think of was Grant. And the missing diary.

The rest of the day took place in slow motion. At six that evening, Grant walked into the station from the Fifth Street entrance. Coming out of the chief's offices, Andrea spotted him.

He didn't see her for a second, and in that silent moment, as she studied him, her heart seemed to constrict. He was dressed in black slacks and a gray dress shirt, his muscular body coiled and tense. What would it be like, she wondered again, to have a man like that love her?

He turned his head in her direction and their eyes met. Her heart squeezed even tighter.

In two short strides, he was by her side. He put his hands on her shoulders and a shiver went through her. He spoke in an undertone that no one else could hear. ''Dulcet's going to meet us at eleven tomorrow night. At Vicki's house. I wasn't sure he was going to go for it at first, but he came through.''

When she didn't answer, he looked at her closer. She knew she wore a stricken expression and his eyes seemed to darken as they took it in.

''What's wrong?'' he asked, his fingers pinching her shoulders. ''What is it?''

''Someone broke into my house,'' she said grimly.

"I don't even know when it happened or how, but it did. They took the diary, Grant. It's gone."

ANDREA HAD to get through the remainder of her shift before they could really talk. Grant agreed to return at six the following morning and they made arrangements to meet at a coffee shop down the street.

The hours dragged. With one eye on the clock and her mind spinning, Andrea found sleep impossible that night. She lay on her bunk and willed a call to come in. Dispatch stayed silent, however, and at 4:00 a.m., she got up.

By the time the rest of the crew woke, she had breakfast ready. They always razzed her about her less-than-perfect cooking skills, and this morning proved no exception. She took in the teasing and responded appropriately, even cleaning up afterward, her anxiety growing the whole time. Finally, Nate and Pete, her shift's replacements, arrived. The two men were barely in the door when she took off.

Grant was waiting at the diner as promised.

She slid into the leather booth. "God, I've been counting the minutes," she said. "I'm so worried—"

He took her hands in his and held them steady. "Take a deep breath and calm down. You're too rattled."

"You would be too—"

He tightened his grip on her fingers. "I mean it. Close your eyes and take a deep breath."

She did as he instructed. Then she felt his thumbs begin to massage her wrists. The simple touch was more than she needed to send her mind stumbling in a different direction. She opened her eyes because she didn't want to go there. Sometime in the middle of the night, she'd realized how fast they were heading for disaster. She wanted Kevin. He wanted Kevin. The poor kid couldn't be split in two, so one of them was going to lose. She was pretty sure it'd be Grant, too. He had no biological ties to the boy and the court would certainly consider that, but would that be best for Kevin? Under those circumstances, what chance did she and Grant have of maintaining any kind of relationship?

Freeing her hands from his, Andrea avoided his eyes and signaled the waitress for juice. She felt his puzzled look but ignored it and by the time the woman came to the table carrying a glass and a pitcher, he'd apparently decided to let the moment slide. For now.

"Tell me what happened," he demanded.

She filled the tumbler and took a long swallow, then spoke slowly. "After we went to the beach with Kevin, I drove directly home. I didn't notice anything out of the ordinary. The door was locked, the windows were closed…everything seemed perfectly fine. I went to bed. The next morning I decided I should take the diary with me in case I might not have time to go back later and get it.'' She topped off her juice and looked up. ''I had hidden it in a container I keep under my bed. It wasn't there.''

''Did you look—''

She stopped him with a weary shake of her head. ''Believe me, Grant, I looked everywhere. It's not there. Someone came into my house and got it. Dulcet, I would guess.''

''I don't think so.''

''No one else would want it and he's—''

''Andrea, if Dulcet had the diary, he wouldn't have agreed to meet us.''

''But who else would want the damn thing?''

''Lots of folks.'' He told her about seeing the men go into Dulcet's office. ''Another politician who wants to run in his place, other girlfriends, the trust people, an overenthusiastic employee…''

''But how would they have known about Vicki, much less the diary?''

''Vicki could have told someone about the affair—maybe she had a friend, someone she trusted but shouldn't have—and they told a friend and they told a friend…'' Grant played with a spoon, tapping it against the table for a moment. ''There's always the obvious, too. If we're wrong and Dulcet didn't murder Vicki then the real killer could have the damn thing. That's not impossible, you know.''

For some reason, Andrea thought of the woman who had visited the house just after the funeral, but her brain was so frazzled she couldn't even remember her name right now. She raised her eyes to Grant's, her voice full of dejection. "So what are we going to do?"

"Exactly what we were going to do before this happened," he said flatly. "Dulcet doesn't have the diary, but he doesn't know we don't, either. We'll fake it and see what happens."

THEY WALKED down Bright Street to the lot where Andrea had parked her Jeep. Along with the traffic, the heat was building, shimmers of it skipping along the sidewalk ahead of them. The unrelenting temperature seemed ominous to Grant. He wasn't the kind of cop who paid attention to so-called instincts, but something in the hot, dead air felt wrong. He wanted to convince himself it had nothing to do with Andrea's news, yet he couldn't help but wonder.

What in the hell was going on? Who had that diary?

As they drew close to her SUV, Grant decided his uneasiness might have more to do with Andrea than it did with the meeting tonight. She was edgy and wired, almost standoffish.

They got to her Jeep, and she hit her remote to unlock the vehicle. She started to open the door, but Grant put his hand on the scorching metal and held it shut. Her questioning eyes met his.

"What's wrong?" he said bluntly. "You aren't acting like yourself."

"Everything's wrong, that's what," she said defensively. "Who could act normal with this going on?"

"Dulcet doesn't scare you. And it's not the missing diary, either. I can tell."

Her expression went rigid and she started to lie to him—he could see it—then she seemed to change her mind.

"I'm worried about Kevin," she said.

"He's going to be fine. The doctors—"

"That's not what I meant, Grant."

The world shrank to the space that separated the two of them.

"How are we going to work everything out without someone getting hurt?"

Grant pondered her question, then he found himself reaching for her. He wanted to freeze the moment forever, to etch it in his mind. The feel of her skin, the fragrance of her perfume, the sweet, sweet tenderness of her skin.

He brought his lips to hers and kissed her for as long as he dared, finally pulling back.

"It's *not* going to work out," he said. "Someone *will* get hurt and there's no way around it."

CHAPTER SIXTEEN

WAITING FOR GRANT to pick her up later that evening, Andrea sat on the couch and repeated his earlier words.

Someone will get hurt.

"You're right," she whispered. "Dammit, you're right...."

She didn't want to think that someone might be her, but strangely enough, she didn't want Grant to suffer that fate, either. There didn't seem to be an answer.

Believing she heard the Impala, Andrea turned to part the front blind with two fingers. The street was empty and she sat back down, her nerves rattling anxiously. She'd heard noises all evening, from scratches against the windows to taps on the sides of the house. She was creeping herself out.

Without any warning, Vicki's image suddenly materialized in Andrea's memory.

Would Vicki approve of what Andrea and Grant were about to do? She'd loved that rat Dulcet, apparently until the bitter end. How would she feel knowing they were about to set him up?

Andrea had no idea because her sister had turned out to be a stranger. An even bigger one, it seemed, than Grant. She closed her eyes and thought once more of their love-making. She was such a fool for letting that happen.

A knock sounded at the front door.

"It's me, Andrea. Grant. Open up."

She unlocked the door and Grant came inside. Embracing at once, they kissed deeply then walked through the house and into the garage where they climbed into Andrea's Jeep. His coat fell open in the process and she saw that he wore a gun.

"Do you think you need that?" Her eyes dropped to the holster.

"I hope not but I *was* a Boy Scout. It's good to be prepared."

She echoed his sentiment then put the SUV in gear. A few cars were out but mainly the streets were empty. This late, Courage Bay usually shut down. Andrea wondered about the homes they passed, lamps lit behind closed curtains, families preparing for bed. The Norman Rockwell images lingered until they reached the bungalow. At that point, reality returned. Grant ducked beneath the windows of the Jeep to slide out of sight.

"Pull into the garage and let me out, then go back and park in the driveway. He wanted you to

meet him, not me. We can't let him know I'm anywhere near.''

Walking quickly up the sidewalk a few minutes
later, Andrea wondered if there were eyes on her
back. She felt them, but her imagination had been
running wild all night and she knew she could be
imagining the sensation. Letting herself inside, she
traversed the empty home in the darkness. She'd
turned off the electricity per Grant's instructions the
day they'd decided on their plan.

She opened the door to the garage, and he slipped
inside like a shadow. A breath away, he spoke, his
lips brushing her ear.

''It's going to be okay.''

THEY'D BEEN WAITING almost an hour when Grant
heard a car outside. He signaled to Andrea to get
her attention, but she'd heard it, too. Frozen on the
other side of the room, she jerked her eyes to his
then she stood and moved to the window, her ap-
pearance Dulcet's sign. The street lamp outside
framed her silhouette and suddenly, Grant wanted
to drag her back, out of the light.

He was too late, though.

A moment after she stepped in front of the glass,
a set of headlights slowed and stopped at the curb,
then went out. A door thudded shut, and in the still
night air, measured footsteps reverberated on the
sidewalk. Grant slid out of sight into the darkened

hallway, glancing to his right. The setup was perfect. All he had to do was look at the mirrored wall in the dining room and he could see everything.

They'd left the front door unlocked. Dulcet pushed it open and walked in, carrying a small duffel.

Even if Grant had been unable to see the senator in the mirror, he would have still known the man's reaction upon seeing Andrea. Dulcet's sharp intake of breath and muttered curse gave him away.

"I'll be damned.... You...you look just like her."

"I've been told that," Andrea answered. "But don't think it means I act like her."

He studied her for a long time and Grant wondered what was going through his mind. Did it feel strange to see someone so similar to his dead mistress now standing before him, alive and well?

Dulcet dropped the bag and crossed the room to where she stood. "Vicki had the good sense to leave Corbin. If you're in this with him, you're keeping bad company."

"I disagree, but I have the feeling you and I might disagree about a lot of things."

The hair on the back of Grant's neck rose as Dulcet drew a finger down Andrea's cheek. She froze and Grant moved his hand to the grip of his holstered weapon.

"Sometimes disagreements can be…stimulating."
Dulcet's voice was low and smooth, but there was
something off about it. "Dissent can lead to inter-
esting compromises, you know."

"Maybe you found that with Vicki," Andrea
said sharply, stepping back. "But I don't believe in
trade-offs. Especially when I have the better hand."

She reached into her jacket pocket and pulled out
the notebook she'd brought with her—the blank
notebook. "I have the diary," she said flatly. "Do
you have the money?"

He hiked a thumb over his shoulder. "It's in the
bag. I'll get it."

"Not yet," she commanded. "First I want you
to tell me what happened. Between you and Vicki
that night. I want to know why you killed my sister."

Grant almost groaned out loud. This wasn't part
of the plan. Dammit to hell, he'd told Andrea to
give Dulcet the notebook and take the money then
let him do the rest.

"I didn't kill her—"

"I'm not a fool, Mr. Dulcet. If you didn't murder
Vicki, you wouldn't be standing here with a duffel
bag full of money."

"Maybe. Maybe not," he replied. "My *career*
would certainly be dead if my constituency ever
found out about the boy, though." He nodded at
the book she held. "That diary has the power to

destroy me. I couldn't get elected dog catcher if this ever came out. In fact, I'd be lucky if the Trust didn't just keep it simple and murder me."

"I thought the Trust backed your political goals…family values and all that."

"The Trust is a huge organization that has its fingers in many pies, Miss Hunt. They wouldn't react well to the news. But let's leave it at that." He smiled unpleasantly. "You know the old cliché—if I told you any more, I'd have to kill you. We don't want that to happen, do we?" His voice hardened. "Hand over the diary."

Grant freed his pistol from the holster and held the weapon at his side.

Andrea spoke calmly. "I'm not giving you anything until you tell me what happened."

Dulcet moved before Grant could react, a pistol suddenly appearing in his hand.

"Stop jerking with me and hand over the damn book." Gesturing with the gun, the senator's grip looked as shaky as his voice. "Right now."

Grant didn't wait to test the man's nerve. Coming around the corner, he steadied his .38 with both hands. "Police," he cried in a loud voice. "Drop your weapon! Drop the gun and get down. Drop it now! Now dammit!"

Dulcet's eyes flicked in Grant's direction but he appeared deaf to the commands. Without any warning, he pulled the trigger.

Andrea screamed and crumpled to the floor.

In the moment that followed, confusion flooded Dulcet's expression, his vacuous gaze locking on Grant in disbelief before it then swung to Andrea's prone body. The enormity of what he'd done seemed to register deep within him.

Grant started forward, but before he could reach Dulcet, the senator raised his gun a second time.

His brains exited the back of his head and splattered the wall where the armoire had been.

SHE FELT COLD AND HOT at the very same time, her stomach rumbling, her shoulder on fire. Outside, sirens wailed but close at hand, all Andrea could hear were the muted voices of what sounded like a hundred people. Alex's face swam into focus. Andrea pushed him away then realized she wanted him closer instead. Her fingers fumbled for his shirt, and when she found it, she pulled him back, straining as she did so to make herself clear. She felt as if she were screaming, but he kept repeating he couldn't hear her. Finally she got him to understand.

"Grant," she croaked. "Is Grant…okay?"

"He's fine." Alex detached her fingers from the front of his uniform and gently placed them on the stretcher. "He's right here and he wants to see you. Not too long, though," he warned. "We need to get you transported ASAP." Stepping back, he put her hand in someone else's.

Her eyes met Grant's and the relief that hit her was as powerful as the pain Dulcet's bullet had delivered. Before she'd fainted, she'd thought of Grant. She'd been sure he was next and the idea of losing him—before she even really had him—had stolen what little breath she'd had left.

She squeezed his fingers and smiled weakly. Then she threw up and passed out.

ANDREA CAME TO in the E.R. The same young intern who'd seen Kevin was now shining a flashlight into her eyes and asking her if she knew where she was. She nodded groggily.

In and out of awareness, she answered a few more questions, then she went for X rays. When she finally came to for good, she was back in the emergency room. The doctor approached with a pan of sterile tools.

"You're a lucky dog," she said. "You've only got a flesh wound and all I have to do is sew this up. I've given you a painkiller and tomorrow you'll be sore, but that should be it. Some antibiotics will do the rest."

Once the sutures were done and the physician gone, Alex and Grant entered, each man wearing identical expressions of concern.

Well, almost identical, Andrea amended. The

look on their faces was not really one and the same. Alex appeared concerned...but Grant seemed terrified. He reached the gurney first and brushed the hair off her forehead, his touch so gentle it made her want to weep. She blamed her reaction on the shot the nurse had given her.

"Are you okay? Are you in any pain? The doctor said the bullet only grazed your shoulder but you lost so much blood—"

Alex broke in, his lopsided grin more relieved than anything else. "Relax, Corbin. She's too damn tough to go down that easy. A .45 might slow her a bit, but not a .22. No way, Jose."

Andrea grinned weakly. "He used a .22? My God, it felt like a cannon." She turned her gaze back to Grant. "Did you get him? Please tell me you arrested Dulcet, Grant...."

He took her fingers in his and the room shrank until she could only see his face and nothing more.

"Dulcet's dead," he said. "Right after he shot you, he turned the gun on himself and ate the barrel. There was no way I could stop him. He's dead...." Grant's eyes turned cold and empty. "And I can't say I'm sorry."

THE HUNTS ARRIVED thirty minutes later, Kevin in tow, all three of them clearly shaken. Over the phone, Grant had tried to reassure them but they couldn't accept that Andrea was all right until they could see for themselves. Grant didn't blame them. When Dulcet had aimed his gun, fear had washed over Grant then rage had swept in.

Three inches to the right and Andrea would have died.

Grant led the Hunts to the cubicle where Andrea lay, then he stepped out of the way. Karen and Jack hurried to the padded table, Kevin between them, wide-eyed and gripping both their hands. Knowing it wouldn't do him any good, but also knowing he couldn't resist, Grant leaned against the back wall and watched the reunion. Karen began to weep and Jack's jaw tightened, their own reaction to what might have been as deep and as painful as Grant's. When Jack lifted Kevin and the little boy threw his arms around Andrea's neck, Grant had to turn away, a swift evisceration removing what was left of his heart. The truth he'd been avoiding since he'd arrived in Courage Bay filled the empty cavity with a hot and heavy pain.

He wasn't needed here. Not by Kevin and certainly not by Andrea.

Kevin had everything a child could possibly require and the chaos of Grant's life would add nothing positive to the situation. Courage Bay—and all it offered—was the place for Kevin, not L.A. On top of all that, what would happen if he and Andrea tried to make a go of it and failed, just as he and Vicki had? Kevin would be devastated.

Grant turned and walked out of the room.

AFTER A QUICK CALL to his office in L.A., Grant went directly from the hospital to the Courage Bay PD. He'd ignored the uniforms at the scene who'd told him to go to the police department instead of the hospital and now it was time to pay the price. The chief of police, a guy named Max Zirinsky, was waiting for him. So was the press. A few TV stations had already caught wind of the situation and Grant had to fight his way through their swelling ranks, repeating "no comment" over and over.

Walking inside Zirinsky's office, Grant had the feeling the chief would have been an all-right guy under normal circumstances. These weren't normal circumstances, though, at least not for Courage Bay. A murder, a shoot-out and a suicide had just taken place on his watch and he wasn't happy. Knowing Andrea, one of his own EMS team members, had been hurt had added to Zirinsky's irritation. Grant's involvement was the capper.

"I suppose you know how deep you're in it?" Without inviting Grant to sit, Zirinsky glared at him from behind his desk. He raised a hand so large it looked like a bear's paw and folded down his fingers as he ticked off his list. "My men ordered you to report here hours ago. You're out of your jurisdiction. You were personally involved with all three victims. You never informed my department or any other official in Courage Bay that any of this was taking place—''

Grant interrupted the sermon. "You don't need to tell me how much I've screwed up, okay?" Reaching into his pocket, he pulled out a business card and tossed it to Zirinksy's desk. "That's my captain's card. I'm with the 04, the Hollenbeck division. His name is Henderson Patton. I've given him some of the details, but he's expecting a call from you.''

The chief glanced at the card then raised his eyes to Grant's. "You already called him?"

Grant nodded.

"You still got a job?"

Grant shrugged. "He didn't say not to show up on Monday.''

"So you're going back to L.A.?"

"Yes, I am.''

"What about your son?"

Grant raised his eyebrows.

"Courage Bay isn't L.A., Detective. We keep a close eye on everyone around here.''

Grant stared out the man's office to the brightly lit fire station next door. "My son will be staying here with the Hunts. It's the best thing for him.''

Zirinsky's measured look told Grant he agreed. He then picked up a pink message slip from his

desk and stood in a dismissive way. Grant took the
hint and started toward the door but Zirinsky's
voice stopped him.

"Not so fast."

His hand on the doorknob, Grant looked over his
shoulder. The chief was holding out the note. "This
is for you. Dulcet's grieving wife has called several
times. She wants to talk to you before you talk to
the press."

"I don't intend to talk to the press."

"Fine by me. She's on her way here, though.
Take my advice and deal with her over the phone
instead of in person. She sounds pretty hard for
someone who has just become a widow."

As Grant's fingers closed on the note, the phone
on the chief's desk rang. Zirinsky picked it up, listened, then put his hand over the receiver. "It's
her," he said. "Are you here?"

Grant nodded and Zirinsky left, closing the door
firmly behind him.

The voice that came over the line was anything
but grief-stricken. Morgana Dulcet seemed wide-
awake and more than alert, her clipped tones so
precise Grant immediately stiffened.

"This is the senator's wife," she said in lieu of
a greeting. "Is this Detective Corbin?"

"This is Corbin."

"I want to know what happened tonight, Detective. But first, I want your reassurance that you have not spoken with the press.''

''I avoid the press whenever possible, Mrs. Dulcet. Keeping them informed is not my job.''

''Good. My people will handle them.'' Her manner was indifferent yet Grant heard the hint of relief in her voice. ''Now please tell me what happened this evening.''

''The chief will talk to you about that, Mrs. Dulcet. The situation is very complicated and—''

''The minute my car pulls up, I'm going to be swamped, Detective. I need to be prepared.'' He heard her say something to someone else, then she came back to him. ''If you think it's too complicated, then let me simplify things. I know who you are and I know who you were married to. I also know about the boy. I know it all, actually, except for what happened tonight. Just fill me in on that and I'll be fine.''

Grant did as she ordered.

''Is she going to live?'' she asked when he finished. ''The sister, I mean.''

''Yes,'' Grant said. It was a curious question to ask first. Another woman in her situation would want more information about her husband rather than the person he had shot. ''Andrea was wounded but not severely. She'll be fine.''

A small thoughtful silence built over the phone before Morgana Dulcet spoke again. ''Then here's what we're going to say." He heard her speak again to someone else instructing them to take notes. "The well-loved senior state Senator Pryor Dulcet took his life tonight in what his constituency will surely see as a tragic end to a very successful career. On the fast track to becoming California's next governor, Dulcet had recently learned he had cancer. While visiting a family friend in Courage Bay, California, he shot himself in despondency over his illness. Arrangements are pending."

Grant's voice went flat. "*Was* your husband ill, Mrs. Dulcet?"

"Yes," she said after a short, distinct pause. "He was. Our family physician will release more information at the appropriate time."

Her plan was crazy. Did she really believe a lie would work? "I don't think you really want to do this—"

Morgana Dulcet interrupted Grant with a voice that could have sliced steel. "This is the truth of my husband's unfortunate demise, Detective Corbin. Any hint, any rumor, any trace of another version will be immediately denounced and the one who spreads the lie will be dealt with appropriately." She paused. "I had lunch last week with the governor, the mayor of L.A. and the police commissioner. I'm sure Chief Zirinsky will see things my way."

He doubted her assessment of Zirinsky, but Grant

no longer cared. ''I think I've got the picture.'' He answered with distraction, his brain suddenly accelerating to warp speed. He didn't like the path it was taking, either.

''Good,'' she said crisply. ''Then I won't expect to hear from you again. Goodbye, Detective Corbin.''

CHAPTER SEVENTEEN

THE DOCTORS DECIDED to keep Andrea for the rest of the night then release her in the morning. After sending her parents and Kevin home, she asked repeatedly about Grant. No one could remember seeing him leave, yet he was gone. Moving her to a room upstairs, the nurses promised they would locate him and send him to her. Andrea tried to stay awake and wait but the sedatives did their job and she went down for the night. When she opened her eyes again, light was streaming through the blinds. The wall clock read 11:00 a.m.

Grant sat in the chair beside the bed.

A storm of emotions assailed her, some so unexpected she couldn't name them, others so powerful they scared her. Grant had not only found the man who'd killed Vicki, he'd also saved Andrea's life. Naturally, her appreciation for what he'd done went beyond words. But the longer she thought about the situation, the more she realized her feelings for Grant went much, much deeper than simple gratitude.

She'd been fooling herself when she'd labeled Grant as another disaster waiting to happen. He *wasn't* the wrong kind of man, for her or for anyone else. He was perfect—kind and intelligent and so sexy she couldn't get him out of her mind.

So why had she thought otherwise?

The answer wasn't flattering.

She'd always gone into her relationships with eyes wide-open. There had been surprises, sure, but she'd actively dated the "mistakes." Her affair with Grant had simply happened...before she could prepare herself. Was there a connection? Had she deliberately been seeking out men all this time who, for one reason or another, weren't right for her? The idea she might engage in such self-destructive behavior shook her badly. Maybe she and Vicki had been more alike than she wanted to admit.

If that was what she'd been doing, here was her opportunity to change. Having Grant in her life could signify a new beginning, a new start. The relationship they'd begun so passionately could develop into something much more...if, and it was a mighty big if, Grant felt the same way. His affection had to be hers and hers alone; Andrea had no intention of sharing her life or her bed with Vicki's ghost.

Her gaze swung to the chair where Grant sat, a kernel of hope growing inside her heart. He was sleeping restlessly, his tall form curled awkwardly in the chair. His hair stood on end as if he'd run his hands through it too many times to count and a rough stubble darkened his cheeks. He hadn't even taken the time to change clothes.

Realizing what that meant—that the rusty stain across his shirt had been made with her blood—Andrea drew in a sharp breath and Grant opened his eyes. Immediately he came to the edge of her bed, taking her fingers in his.

"You're awake," he said. "Tell me how you feel."

"Better than you, I imagine. I got to sleep in a bed last night." She glanced toward the chair, then shook her head, a rush of tenderness coming over her. "You shouldn't have stayed here, Grant. You must be wiped out."

"I am tired," he admitted. "But that's nothing compared to what you've been through. Are you in any pain? Do you need anything?"

She sat up and inventoried her aches and bruises, touching the wide bandage that covered her left biceps. She'd been so engrossed in her emotional upheaval, she hadn't had time to think about her actual wound.

"It's not that bad," she said after a minute. "Vicki accidently whacked me in the shoulder with a baseball bat when we were kids and that hurt more." She paused and gathered herself. "I keep thinking about Vicki. How do you think she would feel about what happened last night?''

''I don't know.'' Grant spoke in a distracted way, his mind obviously not on her question as he moved toward the window. ''I guess she'd be sad. She must have loved the son-of-a-bitch but I'll never know why.''

Andrea eased herself to the edge of the bed. Just as her feet touched the floor, someone knocked softly then opened the door. She looked up to see an aide paused on the threshold, a tray in her hands.

''I thought I heard conversation in here,'' the woman said with a smile. ''Would you like your breakfast now? I had them leave it when they came by earlier and I just reheated it.''

Food was the last thing she wanted, but Andrea smiled and nodded. ''That'd be great. Thank you very much.''

The woman placed the tray on the table beside the bed and left, the smell of coffee and scrambled eggs wafting from the covered plates.

Grant turned back to the window and Andrea went into the bathroom where she washed her face then pushed her fingers through her hair. She wasn't a vain woman but she cringed as her eyes fell on her reflection in the mirror. Vicki would have slit her throat before she'd let Grant see her like this. Since there was nothing else she could do, Andrea simply gave her head another shake and walked back into the room.

She lifted the lid to her breakfast and offered it to Grant but he said ''no thanks'' and returned to what he'd been doing, which was staring out the window. Picking up a piece of toast, Andrea paused. ''I just can't believe how it ended. Dulcet must have felt something for Vicki, but to kill himself like that—''

''He murdered her,'' Grant spoke flatly, his back to Andrea. ''I'm not sorry he's gone.''

Something squeezed her heart, a warning of sorts. ''And the diary?''

''I don't know, but I don't really care, either. Obviously Dulcet killed her. Maybe he had the damn thing all along and just wanted to tie things up by getting rid of us, too.'' Grant's preoccupation continued. *He* was in the room, but his mind wasn't. ''It'll turn up somewhere—at Dulcet's office or his home, whatever.'' He came to the foot of the bed, his eyes on her face. He'd clearly forced away whatever had diverted his thoughts because his gaze was suddenly focused and intense. Andrea felt a second brush of foreboding.

She thrust away her tray, the smell of the food no longer appealing.

''I've decided what I want to do about Kevin,'' he said.

''*You've* decided?'' She kept her voice light, but

her concern only deepened. "No need for any discussion? That's it? You've decided? I would think that Kevin's future is something we all need to have a say in."

His eyes turned so dark, she felt as if she were staring down twin wells. Black, bottomless wells.

"I went by your parents' house early this morning and told them what I wanted to do," he said, ignoring her words. "They agreed with me it'd be for the best and we explained everything to Kevin."

Her pulse jumped. "They agreed with you? I find that hard to believe...unless you've decided to give him up."

He didn't answer. He merely stared.

"Grant?" Her voice rose. "Is that what you're going to do?"

"I can't raise Kevin by myself, Andrea. Your parents can give him so much more, I'd be a fool to take him back to L.A. A selfish fool. He's going to live with them and I'll visit as often as I can." He hesitated, pain etching itself on his face. "I love him too much to take him away from them."

Shock flowed over her and threatened to take her under. This was the last thing she'd expected to happen. The very last thing.

"Y-you're giving him up?" she stuttered. "Just like that?"

"'Just like that' suggests the decision was an easy one. That wasn't the case." His jaw locked with obvious anger. "I've only thought about two things since I came to Courage Bay. Who killed Vicki and what to do about Kevin." As if about to speak again, he took a sharp breath but then he released it, his shoulders slumping.

"No," he amended and raised his eyes to hers. "That's not exactly true. Actually there have been three things."

Andrea's throat closed and she found herself holding her breath.

"You haven't left my mind since the day I got here." He reached out and touched her cheek briefly. "You're a hell of a woman, Andrea, and despite my best intentions not to let it happen, I fell in love with you."

She wanted so desperately to believe him that she almost managed to ignore the caveat she heard in his voice. Almost.

"It stops here, though. If our relationship didn't work out, Kevin would be the one hurt the worst and no matter how much I may want you, I can't do that to him. Nothing means more to me than Kevin." He lifted her fingers to his mouth and kissed them gently, one by one, his gaze meeting hers when he finished, his voice thick as he spoke.

"I'm sorry, Andrea. I love you but I can't afford to be as selfish as Vicki was...and you wouldn't want me if I were."

ANDREA'S PARENTS picked her up from the hospital a little past one. They chattered in the front seat while beside her, in the back, Kevin quietly examined her bandage. She'd told them she could manage on her own, but truth be told, had her Jeep been handy, Andrea wasn't really sure she would have been able to get herself home. Her wound didn't really hurt, but her brain didn't seem to want to work properly.

And why should it? she asked herself in utter disbelief. In the past twenty-four hours, her life had undergone more aftershocks than Orange County had experienced in the past ten years. She'd confronted her sister's killer and been shot in the arm, then she'd realized she'd finally found love—the real kind she'd been hiding from all her life—only to be told it would never work.

They swung by the old house and picked up Andrea's Jeep. Karen drove it home, following behind the others as they returned to Andrea's house. Upon their arrival, her mother fussed in the kitchen until she had a pot of soup going for lunch and her father had clipped the wild jungle out back. After an hour had passed, Andrea convinced them she'd be fine alone and they started out the door. Then her father realized Kevin wasn't with them. He paused at the threshold and looked at the little boy who still stood by the sofa where Andrea sat.

"Come on, Kev. Time to go home."

Kevin's gaze went to Andrea's and she felt a pang in her heart. She'd always thought Kevin's eyes were like Grant's and strangely enough, she still felt that way.

She put her arm around his waist, sensing what he wanted. "Would you like to stay with me tonight?" She patted the cushion on her left. "You could camp out right here on the couch, and then if I needed anything you could help me…"

His eyes rounded and a smile lit up his face. Andrea looked at her father and tilted her head. "Sorry, Dad. We're gonna have a sleep-over."

Jack Hunt started to protest, saying something about her needing her rest, then he stopped so abruptly, she wondered if he knew about her and Grant. Her parents were very sharp people and few things got past them. They hadn't said anything about the relationship but that didn't mean they were in the dark about it—it only meant they were keeping their own counsel.

Which was, she'd begun to realize, something they did a lot. Before Vicki's death, Andrea had known her mother and father had a good relationship but she hadn't really understood how that worked. Now she knew. When one faltered and grew weary, the other one took on the burden. She'd always seen her father as the strong one, yet her mother had just as much strength. And he, in turn, had vulnerabilities she'd only associated with her mother before. They had a wonderful relationship and Andrea suddenly wondered if she'd ever experience that herself.

Her father looked at Kevin. "That what you want?"

Kevin nodded his head so hard, Andrea and Jack both laughed.

"All right, then," her father conceded. "But I'll be by in the morning to get you. We've got some grass to cut in the yard back home. I'm gonna need your help."

He shut the door behind him, leaving Kevin and Andrea alone. Her nephew reached out and carefully touched her bandage, the questions in his eyes making him look concerned. Andrea bided her time. The counselor Kevin had been seeing since he'd come to Courage Bay had told Jack and Karen not to try and guess what Kevin wanted to say. If they continued to do that, she advised, he'd have no incentive to communicate on his own.

Andrea waited. A full minute passed, then the little boy licked his lips and looked at her, one finger still on her arm. "Do...does it hurt?" he asked faintly.

Her heart paused in midbeat. She pulled him to where she sat and lifted him onto her lap. "It stings a bit," she answered. "But it's gonna be fine. I'll be able to swat you in no time at all."

He grinned, completely confident there was no

danger of that ever happening. She hugged him tightly and tucked his head under her chin. "I sure do love you, Kevin. You know that, don't you?"

He nodded but after a moment, he pulled back, a troubled expression on his face. Andrea waited again. This time his words took a little longer to form and when he finally did speak, they were even softer. She had to lean forward to hear him.

"You aren't gonna die, are you?"

She waited for her heart to stop hurting, then she answered him. "No," she said firmly. "I am not going to die. Neither are your grandparents. We're all going to be here a long, long time."

"He died, though."

It took a second for her to understand he meant Dulcet. Kevin had obviously heard some conversations he shouldn't have, she realized.

"He was my father."

Andrea felt her heart crack. "Who told you that, honey?"

"Mommy did." He blinked and looked down at their interlocked fingers. "She said I had to call him 'Father' but I didn't want to. I don't think he wanted me to talk at all." His voice, small before then, disappeared altogether.

She recalled the moment in the hospital when she'd told Kevin he could spend some time with his "father." He'd assumed she'd meant Dulcet. Father/Daddy. Daddy/Father. Who could keep it all straight? Certainly not a six-year-old, that was for sure.

The easiest way to handle the problem had been to simply say nothing.

Andrea wrapped her good arm around the child on her lap, giving him all the comfort she could muster.

He locked his hands behind her neck and gave her the same.

GRANT DIDN'T WASTE any time.

He left for L.A. that afternoon, the Impala moving down the highway as sluggishly as his thoughts. He wouldn't let himself think about the conversation with Andrea or his decision about Kevin because once he headed in that direction, he knew he wouldn't be able to stop, unless it was at the nearest liquor store and even that would be pointless. This pain was too deep to drown. He forced himself to go directly into the station and try and catch up on what had happened while he'd been gone. That proved to be an equally pointless activity but it ate up some otherwise lonely hours.

Stepping inside his stuffy house later Grant dropped his bag in the entry and headed for the kitchen. The images started replaying in his mind, like a movie he'd seen way too often, the senator's final moments flashing behind Grant's eyes. The

soundtrack accompanying the images was the conversation he'd had with Morgana Dulcet.

While he'd been at the hospital with Andrea that
morning, wondering how to tell her he was leaving,
Grant had let his brain get hijacked. It'd been less
painful to think about the case than about them, but
he'd come to an important realization. He'd figured
out why the widow had wanted her late husband's
image to stay intact. Opening his refrigerator, Grant
pulled out a carton of orange juice. The date was
two weeks past, but he drank it anyway.

Morgana had plans to step into Dulcet's size
eleven Cole Haans and take over his political king-
dom. Grant could hear the speech now... Pryor
Dulcet, the man who believed in the family above
all had made the ultimate sacrifice, knowing a quick
death would spare his loved ones. Now she would
sacrifice as well, carrying on his work because no
one else could....

With Dulcet out of the way, Morgana was going
to do what she'd probably wanted to all along—
take over his political career. She might as well,
Grant thought. She'd paid for it, in more ways than
one.

He started to put the carton back in the refrigerator, but then stopped, his fingers tightening on
the container as his mind seemed to implode. Tick-
ing off the points inside his head, he felt his mouth

drop open. Was he thinking straight or had the stress gotten to him?

A dripping sound interrupted his startling thoughts and Grant looked down. He'd gripped the container so hard, it had crumpled and released its contents. A puddle of juice was rapidly spreading on the floor around his shoes.

He stared at the mess for one long second, then he dropped the carton with a curse and whirled on the wet floor, moving so quickly he almost lost his footing. After grabbing the counter to regain his balance, Grant snatched up his keys and ran out the front door.

ANDREA CALLED HER PARENTS that evening and told them about the conversation she and Kevin had shared. They were so thrilled and amazed that Andrea couldn't tell them Kevin had spoken to her before. That would stay a secret for now, just as the reason behind his silence would. No purpose would be served by explaining and it no longer mattered, anyway. Vicki's part in the whole issue would remain unacknowledged. Andrea would tell the boy's therapist everything and they could go from there.

She then called the station. Alex had told everyone what had happened, but Andrea wanted to talk to Ripani herself. The conversation went as she'd suspected it would. She told him she'd be in the following day and Joe had pointed out she couldn't lift anything heavier than an egg.

They finally compromised with her agreeing to take it easy until the following weekend, at which point, she would return and work in the office until her stitches were removed. She hung up knowing that once she was back on the job, she'd be able to finagle her way into the ambulance.

She only wished she knew when her heart would be in one piece again.

Kevin decided on McDonald's for dinner. When the last french fry was gone, they agreed their next stop should be the ice-cream place.

Kevin made his pick quickly. With her chocolate cone and his bubble-gum dip in hand, they strolled back to her Jeep. Rolling down the windows, she drove toward the beach as they enjoyed their final licks. Her cell phone rang a second later, and she pulled over and answered. She couldn't handle a car, an ice-cream cone and a telephone conversation, too.

Her mother sounded harried. "Andrea, I'm so glad I caught you. We've got six people from church coming over for coffee and dessert this evening and I'm baking like a madwoman. A delivery service just called here looking for you, though, so I said I'd track you down and send you over. They have some more of Vicki's boxes, some stuff she had in storage apparently. Can you meet them at the house and let them in?''

Andrea started to question her mother but she wasn't fast enough.

''I've got to run, honey. The cake's about to burn! Talk to you later, okay? Call me if you have any problems...''

Andrea hung up then glanced at Kevin. ''I need to stop by Grandma's old house,'' she said in a matter-of-fact voice. ''It won't take two seconds. Is that okay with you?'' As if she were checking the traffic, she deliberately turned her head while she spoke so she couldn't see him.

''Okay,'' he said.

The one ordinary word thrilled her.

When they pulled up to the curb in front of the bungalow, however, there was no delivery truck in view. Kevin climbed out of the Jeep on his own and clunked up the sidewalk, his walking cast marking his progress. Andrea peered up and down the short street and decided the movers must have gotten tired of waiting and left. Picking up the junk mail from the overflowing box, she shuffled through the flyers and called out for Kevin.

He didn't answer.

With a sigh of exasperation, she dropped the mail in the Jeep then went to look for him. On the front porch, she knew exactly where he'd gone. The door was standing open.

Andrea walked inside, the living room dimly lit by the street lamp outside. She knew instantly that something was wrong but this time the realization required no extra ability on Andrea's part. The trouble was obvious.

Kevin was standing in the middle of the room, a woman Andrea recognized at his side. The last— and only—other time she'd seen her had been here when she'd said her name was Mary Delaware. A cold hard fear paralyzed Andrea as she stared at her now.

The woman had a gun and she was holding it against Kevin's head.

CHAPTER EIGHTEEN

"How are you feeling, Andrea?" Mary Delaware asked. "You look well for someone who's just been shot."

Andrea wanted to scream, but she put the panic into a box deep inside her, her training taking control. She responded as calmly as she would have had the gun been pointed at a stranger's head.

"I don't know who you are or what you think you're doing," she said, "but your problem doesn't involve the boy. Let him go."

"I can't do that," Delaware said. "Because actually he *is* the problem. And you've become one, too. Almost as big a one as your sister."

Andrea's mouth went dry but she managed to speak. "Let him go," she demanded in a low voice. "Then we'll talk about my sister or me or whatever you'd like...."

"We don't need to talk," the woman said.

"Then what *do* you want?"

"I'm here to kill you." Yanking Kevin closer,

Mary Delaware pressed the gun into his temple. "And the boy, too, of course."

Her face a mask, Andrea judged the distance between herself and the woman. Five feet, maybe even six, separated them. Too far for Andrea to leap, even if she hadn't been wounded. Delaware could fire before Andrea would have a chance to push Kevin aside. Andrea's focus returned to the woman as her voice rose another notch.

"...didn't really think I was a friend of your sister's, did you? Do I look like someone who would associate with a person like her?"

Delaware's tone triggered a memory and staring at the woman, Andrea suddenly understood the feeling of familiarity she'd experienced when they had first met.

Her photograph was on the corner of the political poster in Vicki's study.

The ad had been from Pryor Dulcet's latest campaign.

And this woman was Dulcet's wife.

"You're Morgana Dulcet," Andrea breathed.

"Very good. You must have been the smart sister." Morgana lifted her chin. "Now step over to the window and sit down on the floor."

Andrea made no effort to move. "The police will realize who did this," she said quietly. "Killing us will only make things harder on you. You won't get away with it."

"I don't see why not... I did last time."

Andrea's blood went cold. She couldn't move, couldn't think, her entire focus on a single point—Morgana Dulcet's flat and empty gaze.

"You pushed over that armoire, not your husband... You killed my sister."

"Not physically, no. I'm afraid I can't claim that as my own doing. Pryor did it but I had to force him."

Remembering the man's protests, Andrea shook her head in disbelief. "He said he didn't do it."

"Pryor wasn't capable of much, except screwing women he shouldn't have... and lying. He pushed it over all right but I had to practically hold a gun to his head. I'd told him to take care of things before the election got into full swing, but he procrastinated until I threatened to turn off the money. Which I might have had to do, anyway," she added. "Your sister was getting quite expensive. She must have wanted to send the boy to Harvard...."

"The sixty grand," Andrea said numbly.

"Is that all she had left?" Morgana made a tsking sound. "I'd been paying her for months. I would have thought she'd saved a bit more."

"Why were you giving her money?"

"I'd think that was obvious." She dug her fingers into Kevin's shoulders. He winced but kept his silence. "I wanted her to go away but she didn't have the sense to take the money and leave. She wanted Pryor. I couldn't let that happen, though. The revelation of a mistress and a bastard doesn't get a gubernatorial campaign off to a very good start.''

"And murder does?''

"You aren't going to be murdered. There's going to be a tragic explosion attributed to the gas oven and the hot water heater down the hall.''

Now Andrea understood the oven light and the open door to the cupboard holding the water heater. Morgana had been the one who'd broken into this house…and then into Andrea's.

Andrea's hands tightened at her side as she put the pieces together. "You have the diary.''

"Of course I do. I saw it sticking out of your pocket when you came to the door the day I visited.''

"How did you know that's what it was—''

"Please,'' she interrupted Andrea's question. "Your sister was just the kind of person who would pour her little heart out into a book. It was an easy guess…plus Pryor had told me about it.''

"But you didn't let him know you had it?''

"You *are* the clever one, aren't you?'' Morgana smiled slightly, then her expression chilled. "He was becoming useless. I told him before he left to meet you that I didn't want him doing anything silly like shooting himself if things didn't go well, but he didn't listen." She paused. "Then again, I guess I can't really say that, can I? He obviously *did* listen to me…for once."

Her coldness sent Andrea's head spinning. If she had suggested suicide to her husband, Morgana Dulcet would think nothing of killing Andrea and Kevin. Andrea tried one last time. "Grant will figure this out," she said.

"The persistent detective?" she said with disdain. "He's a drunk and a loser, who's going to be looking for work shortly. LAPD doesn't have room in the ranks for someone like him and I'll tell the mayor that. I seriously doubt he'd gain anyone's attention should he decide to talk."

She took the gun from Kevin's head and pointed it at Andrea. "That's all the information you're going to get. Now move to the window and shut up."

TEN MILES OUTSIDE Courage Bay, Grant's cell phone rang sharply. He picked it up with a prayer, hoping to hear Andrea's voice on the other end. He'd called her half a dozen times, leaving messages for her to phone him.

The quivery voice who answered his hello sounded vaguely familiar but it didn't belong to Andrea. Disappointment swamped him.

"Detective Corbin? Is that you? This is Mrs. Moore."

"Yes, Mrs. Moore, this is Detective Corbin. Look, I need to keep my line open—"

"I have something to tell you." She spoke in an undertone, as if she didn't want to be overheard.

"And what would that be?"

"You aren't going to believe what I just saw pull into the garage of the house next door."

"What was it?"

"The black thingie," she said. "You know, the big ole—what'd you call it?—SVU?"

Grant pondered her words for a moment, then his hands tightened on the steering wheel until his knuckles complained. "Do you mean 'SUV'?"

"That's it!" she said. "The big SUV…the same one I saw last time. It pulled up, then went straight into the garage. The door closed behind it." Her voice dropped with disappointment. "I didn't get to see who it was, but not twenty minutes passed when someone else drove up. Guess who?"

"Andrea?"

"That's right! And she had Vicki's son with her."

"Is her car still there?"

"It certainly is." He could hear the rustle of fabric. "I'm looking out the window right now and it's right by the curb."

"Mrs. Moore, I need you to do something for me, okay?"

"You name it," the elderly woman said in an excited whisper. "You got it."

"I want you to call the Courage Bay PD and ask for Chief Zirinsky. Do you need to write down his name or can you remember it?"

"I'm the one who taught *him* how to write it," she sputtered indignantly. "I know who he is!"

"Good, good," Grant answered quickly. "Then call him and tell him I'm five minutes out and I want him to meet me there with a squad in full gear. But silently," he added. "Be sure and say that, okay? No sirens, no lights. That's important."

"I understand," she said. "Anything else?"

"That'll be it for now."

"Okay," she said. "Roger that. Over and out."

ANDREA HELD HER GROUND. "I'll do anything you want," she said, nodding in Kevin's direction, "but not until you release him. He's just a little boy who doesn't understand any of this. Turn him loose, then we'll sort it out."

"I can't chance someone finding out about him."

"Nobody needs to ever find out anything." Andrea heard the note of desperation in her voice. "I won't tell. I'll have his name changed."

"It's not his name that needs to be changed," Morgana replied. "It's his genes. And no one can do that. Sooner or later someone will uncover his father's identity and the press will go berserk."

Kevin tensed under the woman's grip and she looked down at him. "You know who I'm talking about, don't you? Your mother told you everything."

He stayed silent and stared at her.

She shook him slightly. "Answer me, young man."

Andrea willed Kevin to look at her but his gaze was fixed on Morgana. "He doesn't talk," Andrea said. "He won't answer you."

Morgana raised her eyes in surprise. "He's mute?"

Andrea paused as if thinking over her answer. The longer she could keep Morgana talking, the more time it gave her.

"He isn't mute," she replied. "He just doesn't talk."

Morgana tilted her head. "I believe that's the definition of being mute, isn't it? When one doesn't talk, one is mute?"

"He's capable of speaking but he doesn't." Her eyes slid around the darkened room. There had to be a weapon of some sort lying around, a leftover piece of wood, a scrap of glass…something. The adrenaline shooting through Andrea's veins made up for any deficit her wounded arm might have caused.

Morgana didn't notice when Andrea moved another step nearer.

"Has he always been that way?"

In the process of taking a second step, Andrea froze. "It's a recent development actually."

"He just stopped talking?"

"Basically."

"Why?"

"We aren't quite sure."

The questions continued as Morgana turned back to Kevin with a curious look. As she spoke, the little boy cut his eyes to Andrea. She frowned and shook her head slightly and he nodded with an almost imperceptible move, clearly understanding that she didn't want him to say anything. Andrea didn't know what but she had to do something and do it quick. If she didn't, they were both going to die.

Five minutes later, all hell broke loose.

THE FRONT DOOR BURST OPEN and so did the back, the heavy slabs of oak simultaneously crashing into the stucco behind them with shrieks that sounded like screams. Grant rushed into the living room with five men behind him and two seconds later, Zirinsky's team came in from the rear.

Grant knew what to expect—as in any SWAT operation, they'd used mirrors to look inside—but he still wasn't prepared for the spasm of pure terror that hit him. He swallowed back a surge of bile, his breath coming in short spurts and stared in disbelief. Morgana Dulcet stood in the center of the room with a gun to Kevin's head. Andrea was poised by the window, pale and sick with obvious helplessness.

The team swarmed in behind him, and Grant raised his weapon with stiff arms, screaming, "Drop it! Drop the gun!"

Advancing as he yelled, Grant was a single step from Morgana when Andrea lunged past him. With a wild cry, she knocked Morgana off her feet, the pistol she'd held clattering to the floor.

Using the distraction as Andrea had known he would, Grant quickly holstered his gun and thrust Kevin behind his body, protecting him as best he could. Another set of hands then snatched the child away.

Grant dropped on top of the two women as they grappled for Morgana's gun. Despite her wound, Andrea was younger and in much better shape, but it was her righteous anger that made the difference.

On her hands and knees, she reached for the gun just as Grant grabbed Morgana's arms. Swatting at the barrel with the tips of her fingers, Andrea sent the pistol spinning into the nearest corner. With a gasp, she lost her balance, then tumbled, falling on her side, her scream of pain piercing the confusion. Grant managed to wrestle both of Morgana's arms behind her back, Zirinsky's men joining the fight. Her clothes torn, her sleek hair mussed, she cursed and kicked but they easily subdued the now hysterical woman and dragged her from the room, her cries of outrage echoing in the hot night air.

Grant stumbled to Andrea's side. She'd managed to get back up on her hands and knees, but she was swaying, blood running down her arm from underneath her bandage.

Just as he reached her, Andrea lifted her head and spoke in a hoarse voice.

"Clear...the house and check...the...oven," she rasped. "I think it's set to blow."

GRANT'S DARK EYES FLARED with shock but he didn't hesitate. "Clear the house," he screamed. "Clear the house. She opened the gas valves!"

For one heart-stopping second, the cops all froze then a controlled frenzy took over. Passing on the cry, they scrambled out any exit they could find, some even diving out the windows.

Grant moved just as quickly. Helping Andrea stand, he tried to drape her good arm around his shoulders, but a wave of dizziness swamped her and halfway up, she felt herself crumple back to the floor. Grant fell to his knees and picked her up then raced for the front door.

They made it across the street just as the house exploded.

IT SEEMED AS IF debris fell out of the sky forever, but in reality, the whole thing was over in seconds.

An hour later, though, Andrea was still shaking. Holding Kevin close, she let Rhonda check them both for injuries then rebandage her wound. Rhonda then turned her attentions to Grant, peppering Andrea with a barrage of questions as she swabbed his minor cuts and bruises.

Andrea answered the ones she could, then held up her hand. "You're gonna have to wait for another day," she said. "I've got to catch my breath!"

Rhonda arched a dark eyebrow and slapped a square of gauze on the back of Grant's neck where a small piece of glass had hit him. "All right," she said, "but I expect to hear every little detail as soon as this is over. I have the feeling you've been holding out on me...."

Grant winced and Andrea promised. Rhonda and Kevin then headed to where Mrs. Moore was passing out cookies in her front yard. Grant and Andrea sank to the curb and looked at each other.

Soundlessly, he wrapped his arm around her waist and she reached over to take his hand, their embrace now a complete circle. The feeling was a welcome one, but it didn't cure her trembling. In fact, she felt another wave of dizziness hit her. She was pretty sure this one had nothing to do with her head and everything to do with her heart, but Alex appeared a moment later and she didn't have time to consider what that meant.

Kneeling before them, he took off his helmet and swiped his brow. "You guys were incredibly lucky," he said. "You ought to go buy Lotto tickets today...."

Grant tilted his head toward the house. "Was luck all that kept it from blowing earlier?"

"She'd only cracked the valve on the stove but sooner or later, it would have gone."

He reached into his pocket and tossed a six-inch strap of plastic to Grant.

Grant looked at it and then at Alex.

"Dulcet's wife had them in her pocket. One of Zirinsky's guys gave it to me." Alex turned at Andrea. "She was going to tie you and Kevin up, then really open up the juice right before she left."

"Why didn't it go up before?"

"No spark and not enough gas. When you guys got there—" he nodded toward Grant "—you opened all the doors and a lot of what had leaked out then escaped. When the fumes finally hit the hot water heater down the hall, though, that was all it took." He looked back at the blown-out windows and damaged roof. One side of the rear of the house had a huge hole in it, too.

"You're lucky," he repeated, almost as if warning them. "Very, very lucky..."

Alex walked away and Grant turned to Andrea. "He's got that part right. We *are* lucky, lucky as hell." He pulled her even closer and kissed her deeply. "Are we going to take advantage of that or let it pass us by?"

Andrea found herself holding her breath. She let it out slowly. "I guess that depends...." She lifted her eyes to his. "What did you have in mind?"

"I have no idea," Grant said. "But whatever it is, it won't involve leaving Courage Bay." He paused. "Or leaving you and Kevin."

She told herself to stay calm. "What are you saying, Grant?"

"I'm saying what I should have weeks ago." His eyes locked on hers and his hand tightened on her hip. "I love you, Andrea. You're a very special woman and I don't want to lose you before I even have you."

"What about L.A.? What about your job?"

"L.A.'s not going anywhere and neither is the job." He grinned and her heart skipped several beats. "When Kevin's ready for college, we'll go back."

She caught the *we,* yet felt as if she had to warn him regardless.

"I don't have a very good track record with relationships," she said.

"That's only because you haven't had one with me."

He kissed her again, and this time, she felt it everywhere.

"Are you sure?" she had to ask.

"Hell, no, I'm not sure." He shook his head and stared at her. "Who can be sure about anything? Look at what almost happened! When I walked in that room and saw you and Kevin, I nearly came unwound, right then and there. I've never had that feeling before." He looked across the street at the wrecked house, then focused on her again. "You don't come that close to losing people you love without realizing what that means. I love you. And you know I love Kevin. I want to work it out somehow—you, me, him. Will you give us a chance?"

She held his gaze with her eyes. "You two are the reason I came back to Courage Bay. I just didn't know it at the time." She then pulled Grant to her and kissed him one more time, a single thought running through her head.

Those people were wrong.

You *could* go home again.

You just had to know where home really was.

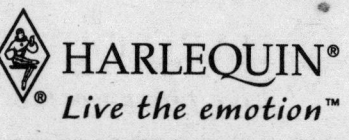

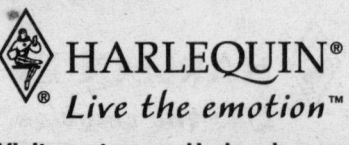

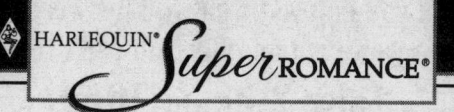

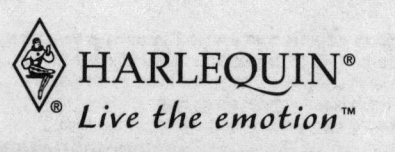

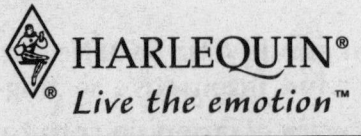

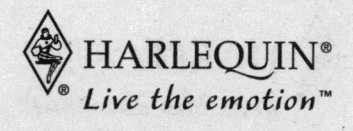

Forrester Square

LEGACIES . LIES . LOVE .

Secrets and romance unfold at Forrester Square…
the elegant home of Seattle's most famous families
where mystery and passion are guaranteed!

Coming in June…

BEST-LAID PLANS

by

DEBBI RAWLINS

Determined to find a new dad, six-year-old Corey Fletcher takes advantage of carpenter Sean Everett's temporary amnesia and tells Sean that he's married to his mom, Alana. Sean can't believe he'd ever forget such an amazing woman…but more than anything, he wants Corey to be right!

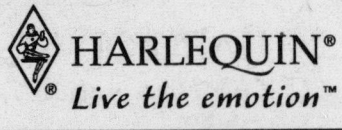

HARLEQUIN®

Live the emotion™